*Worlds Collide by Karen Wiesner*

# Worlds Collide,
## Book 6: Family Heirlooms Series

### *Newly Revised and Reissued!*

## by Karen Wiesner

**Awards & Honors:**
*5 hearts and Sweetheart Award winner from
The Romance Studio
5 stars from MyBookAddiction Reviews*

**ISBN:** 978-1-312-32901-0 (trade paperback)
**Copyright © 2014 by Karen Wiesner**
**http://www.karenwiesner.com**
*Original copyright © 2012, Second Edition*

Electronic formats coming soon from
http://www.writers-exchange.com/Karen-Wiesner.html

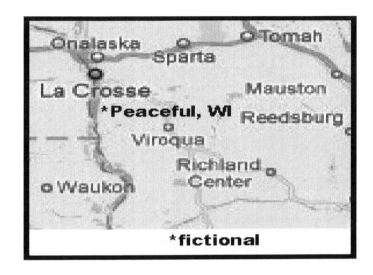

# Family Heirlooms Series:

*Nuggets of faith can be passed down as family heirlooms from parent to child, sibling to sibling, spouse to spouse.*

### Book Six Family Heirloom: Persevering in adversity

# Chapter 1

*In twelve years of being in this country, I've become a human bobble head—and not a very authentic Japanese one,* Dr. Marcus Samuels thought as he passed colleagues and gave the customary bow of respect at meeting in the hall. In the United States, polite though sincere head inclinations of greeting or acknowledgement were routinely exchanged, but nothing like the humble, deferential form he'd learned to give everyone in an effort to avoid trouble since arriving in Japan. He'd never been particularly good at the custom.

In the relief of an empty hall in front of him, Marc wasn't sure why the practice suddenly made him slightly irritable and all but limp with fatigue. His shift at the hospital had been long, true, and he'd gotten little sleep the night before. In the end, he knew the core of his stress. Since he'd sent that ultimatum last night to Dan, the program coordinator of the Worldwide Medical Ministry Organization, a weight had settled on his chest. The situation had been in the back of his mind every minute of this day. Despite believing he had no other choice, Marc didn't "do" ultimatums often...or particularly well. *And now I either return to my apartment and get the answer I demanded, or I face another bout of Dan's endless runaround. The man excels at avoidance. Regrettably, I've been too malleable up to this point. No more.* Marc raised his pleading gaze heavenward. *Dear Lord, no more.*

Abruptly, a colleague turned the corner directly in front of him. His gaze morphed into something between a hasty pulling together of himself and a bow. The nurse gave him an odd look as they passed each other, and Marc glanced back to see her disappearing around the next corner. He couldn't help chuckling to himself. At the rate he was going, the last impression he gave those he worked with at the hospital wouldn't be a good one. *Not at all.* He was losing his sanity, and he knew that going home and staying where he belonged indefinitely was the only thing that could cure him.

Marc had joined the WMMO at a point in his life when he'd been rebelling against following the pattern set by everyone else in his family. His parents and siblings had given their lives to Christ, settled down to marriage and families, and served God where they were. They were all homebodies, and, unfathomably in retrospect, Marc had convinced himself he could be different. With most of his medical education, certification and training completed, he'd joined WMMO's post-residency program when he was twenty-eight, believing he was ready to see the world and serve the Lord wherever he was sent. His life had looked shiny and new...

He'd stepped off the plane in Nagasaki and instantly had the first of many panic attacks that quickly led to an all-out panic disorder. *Talk about worlds colliding.* He'd realized at that moment he was even *more* of a homebody than anyone else in his family. Unfortunately, he couldn't change his mind. He'd committed himself to five years in the program. If not for Haruki Oichi, who'd taken him under his wing when he'd arrived, Marc was certain he wouldn't have survived. Somehow he'd gotten through the time, and Haruki had convinced him to stay on longer than even that. Then Haruki's younger sister, Keiko, had arrived five years ago and Marc had wondered if his supervisor had planned that, too. Keiko had settled Marc in a way he could never have expected, and he'd stayed on long past his initial commitment.

In total, twelve years had passed. A series of family crises—his oldest brother's wife had died, his baby sister had been raped, and, most recently, his youngest brother's wife's miscarriage—along with multiple celebrations that he'd missed almost completely, had brought him to an unwavering decision. He was going home. For good. He'd prayed about it, of course, but he'd made up his mind and nothing would change it.

When he'd announced his resignation to Dan, he supposed he shouldn't have been surprised at how his supervisor had hemmed and hawed, throwing more reasons at him to stay. Eventually, Dan had sent a replacement that Marcus and the rest of the field team had been training for the past month. Because the doctor wasn't fully instructed in a program of this type, Dan had asked Marc to stick around a little longer. *Like an idiot, I have, too. But last night I gave my ultimatum. My final word. I'm going home. I'm giving up missionary work. I have every intention of becoming a daily fixture in my family's lives. And maybe I'll finally get married and start a family of my own.*

In and of itself, the latter goal was a daunting task. He was forty years old. Any romantic prospects he'd entertained at home were long gone. In truth, he hadn't dated much in the last few years. How could anyone else...anyone but Haruki and Keiko...understand that he'd given his life to the medical missionary field and yet he'd spent twelve years almost completely out of his element in this country? Leaving Japan, he'd accepted, would mean starting his life over from scratch. *Daunting? Try exhausting. No wonder I can't sleep lately.*

"Marc-*san*," someone called behind him.

Recognizing Haruki's voice, Marc halted and turned around. Like many of the Japanese men he'd met, Haruki Oichi was small—barely five foot six with short, well-trimmed, black hair and dark eyes. From the first, Marc had felt like a giant next to the island natives. At six foot, he was tall but not unduly so by American standards. Here, he was Gulliver—and he'd discovered the shock of that the first time he'd tried to buy clothing and shoes in this country. Now he went home once or twice a year and bought new clothes then, if he needed them.

Marc waited for Haruki to catch up to him, then gave a twenty-degree bow, slightly to the side so as not to bump heads with his friend. Keiko and Haruki were fellow pediatricians at the Children's Christian Mission Hospital and both were also part of WMMO's post-residency program. They'd grown up in the States as foreign exchange students and given their lives to Christ during that time.

"Come, friend, have dinner with Keiko and myself in the cafeteria."

Marc offered a smile. "Not tonight, Haruki. Long day."

"What else is new?" Haruki raised an amused eyebrow.

"New? I've got some calluses I'd like to stop walking on."

Haruki grinned. "Dinner. Then your calluses can call it a night."

"No. Not tonight, friend. Some other time, all right?"

Haruki allowed him to beg off with the common

phrase *"Otsukaresama deshita"* ("You're tired"), and
Marc continued out of the hospital and across the
campus to the WMMO resident housing dorms. He was
about to enter the ground elevator and take the car up
to his floor when Keiko Oichi burst through the
double-door entrance of the building. At thirty-three,
she looked more like a young girl. He'd never met a
woman more petite than she was. She was barely five-
five and, on appearances alone, Marc didn't believe she
could be more than ninety-five pounds. That said,
there was nothing child-like about her. Her face was
delicately exquisite, exotic, her hair shiny and jet
black, worn in a classic chignon during her hours on
duty at the hospital. Silken strands framed her tiny
face, giving her a look that was both waifish and
elegant. Off-duty, she wore her hair loose, down past
her shoulders. To Marc, she was impossibly more
beautiful that way with her golden skin, exotic black
eyes and full, wide mouth set against white teeth and
her tiny, China doll face.

Marc smiled warmly as she approached him
wearing a sophisticated pencil skirt and a silk top
under her open lab coat. "My brother tells me you can't
be persuaded to have dinner with us."

Because he couldn't hide anything from her, he
admitted, "I'm waiting for an e-mail."

"From Dan?"

He nodded, and he knew looking into her beautiful
eyes that she guessed everything he didn't say.

"Did you give him the ultimatum?" she asked.

"In no uncertain terms."

She giggled, obviously aware that he was teasing
when he made it sound like he and their supervisor
had duked it out with pistols at dawn. "Good. But you
know Dan will wait as long as he possibly can before

responding."

That was true. And Marc wasn't so sure he could hold himself together if he checked his e-mail and didn't find a response of any kind from Dan.

"Have dinner with us and then you can check, Marcus-*san*. I'll come with you so you can have someone there when you open your e-mail."

*That would make me feel better. I'm tired, but...* In five years, Marc hadn't been able to deny Keiko Oichi a thing. She slipped her arm through his and led him back to the hospital, through the maze of seemingly endless halls to the cafeteria. Before he even fully stepped inside the gymnasium-sized room, he saw a huge sign with the words "Bon Voyage, Dr. Samuels" and the Japanese equivalent below. The cafeteria was filled with everyone he knew at the hospital.

At the front, Haruki grinned at him, shaking his head. "I should have known Keiko could convince you," he explained his amused disbelief.

Marc acknowledged sheepishly that *he* should have known Keiko would throw him a going-away party...and he understood why she'd done it—done it *now*—too. Before anyone else, Keiko knew best that he wanted to go home, and this party would make him see that he really was finished here. It would provide closure for him. If she'd waited to throw it for him just before his "ultimatum leave date" at the end of the month, he might have given in to Dan's hedging yet again. Marc had wondered a time or two if Dan guessed that he wasn't exactly sure the Lord was guiding him in this departure. His supervisor knew just what to say to get him waffling in his decisions. *But not this time.*

Squeezing Keiko in a one-armed hug of gratitude, Marc let her lead him into the circle of colleagues and friends he'd made over the past twelve years.

"You must have put that together pretty fast," Marcus commented as Keiko rode the elevator with him up to his floor in the male dormitory. "Today? During your shift?"

Keiko raised an eyebrow mysteriously. "I have friends in high places," she claimed.

Just as she'd hoped, Marcus laughed in the deep baritone that always sent a shiver of pleasure down her spine. She could happily listen to him laugh for the rest of her life. *And watch,* she decided after a surreptitious peek at him. Whenever Marcus laughed or smiled, deep grooves—dimples—bracketed his full, firm mouth. Without a doubt, she found him almost otherworldly attractive. He was tall in a way she'd rarely experienced in her life, even after growing up, for the most part, in the United States. He also worked out regularly in the gym and he was muscular and well-formed like males in pictures of mythological Greek gods.

Her arm was linked with him, and he pulled her a little closer, hugging her slightly as his hazel eyes gazed into hers. Marcus was always direct. That trait was one of the endless things that had drawn her to him.

"Thank you, Keiko. You always know just what to do and when to do it. It was just the kick in the pants I needed."

She couldn't help giggling, covering her mouth with her hand as she did so. Marcus grinned again, and she felt a familiar tug deep inside her chest. *Marcus is leaving. He won't be talked out of it this time—and I made sure of it with the party, which I suspected would solidify his decision prompting that e-mail to Dan last night. I did it to make him happy. I don't regret it. But what will I do when he leaves?*

The sensation that flooded her was like a great black hole opening up in front of her and sucking her inside with a tremendous force she couldn't resist. Luckily, the ancient elevator gave a slight lurch and Marcus, ever the protective male, grasped her a little tighter to him to steady her. Shyly, she smiled up at him. "So, you're determined not to let Dan talk you out of leaving this time?" she asked softly.

"It's time."

Yes, she'd sensed the same. Marcus had committed to the WMMO program before he'd truly understood what he was getting into—how he would be affected by living so far from home and for so long. Dan had been a master at finding just the right incentive to ground Marcus—right where he needed him. But after twelve years, those incentives were no longer enough to keep Marcus from his heart's desire. Going home and never leaving again had been driving him relentlessly of late. Nothing beyond a force of nature or the Lord's divine intervention could change his end game now.

Marcus let her go to unlock the door of his apartment. After she'd gone inside before him, murmuring "*O-jama shimasu*" ("sorry for disturbing"), she quickly stepped out of her comfortable work shoes and into the indoor slippers Marcus provided for her visits. He was already turning her shoes around and putting them together so she could slip into them easily when it was time for her to leave.

She couldn't help thinking about all the things he'd

learned since coming here—customs and manners that had been difficult for him to adopt because she understood that they felt unnatural, sometimes even unnecessary, to him. For Marcus, the idea of being forced to wear slippers, especially communal ones, inside the house was foreign. If he wasn't worried about offending someone, she didn't doubt that he'd walk around barefoot all the time. That was only one of many strange rituals he'd conceded to uneasily. He rarely spoke of his feelings, but she'd come to know him well in five years. She believed growing up in the West had given her insights into him that she never would have had if she hadn't become what she very privately considered half Japanese and half American.

Often, she'd wondered if Marcus could comprehend how difficult life was for her in this place, even more so than it'd ever been for her brother, though he'd also grown up in the United States. If her family knew how much of an individual she'd become, they would be horrified and disappointed in her. She'd worked doubly hard to maintain her *aisatsu* (proper greetings and behaviors). Naturally, she didn't want to come off as foolish, improper or ill-bred, but, even more than that, she didn't want anyone to know how different she was from other Japanese women.

"Tea?" Marcus suggested.

She nodded, thanking him. While he went to the tiny kitchen section of the studio apartment, she immediately strode to his compact iPod speaker system and programmed their current favorite classical music. They always listened to it loud. "You can't listen to classical any other way", they'd often said in unison when there were complaints from fellow dorm-mates.

She sat down on her knees in front of the *kotatsu*

table, glancing around the room with a sense of nostalgia. Marcus had done very little to decorate his room and hadn't seen the point of partitioning off spaces for rooms, which, to him, would have made the apartment even smaller than it already was. She also realized anew how few possessions he had. Even after twelve years in the same place, he insisted on not collecting more than he needed to be comfortable. Keiko had understood from the first time she'd met him that that was part of his panic disorder. He wanted to be able to leave this place at a moment's notice. He kept no more than what could fill two suitcases and a small carryon. Instead of books, which he loved, he'd bought an electronic reader that held all the reading material he needed. His music was in the company iPod system. One of the first times she and Marcus had gotten together after she'd arrived at the hospital, he'd told her that, until he'd moved to Japan, he'd had little if any skill with electronics or technology. He'd learned because it was a way to live sparingly that would allow him to pack up and flee in mere minutes.

Marcus was different, as different as Keiko felt herself to be. She'd often noticed that Haruki considered Marcus-*san* one of his closest friends, but even he couldn't quite understand him. Her brother didn't understand Marcus's desire to make everyone part of his family—and to create a family for himself in the process. He didn't understand Marcus's underlying nervousness about being in a foreign country that included none of the comforts he was used to—rich food, conveniences, the ability to relax and accept everyone as they were. *To be able to put cream and sugar in his tea if he wants to and not offend someone for doing so.*

With a rush of unusually tender emotion, she watched him prepare the tea. *I'm so foreign, too. Maybe I wouldn't have been if Haruki hadn't begged our parents to let me join the foreign exchange program when I was a young girl. Maybe I would have accepted my life for what it was without thought or consideration for what I truly wanted for myself. I would have mindlessly become what my family expected me to be because it's not the Japanese way to question how things are, to question the group-mind. I would have done my duty out of a sense of giri, the burden of obligation every single Japanese child is instilled with from birth, and to keep the harmony. But now, in part because I've accepted Christ and I have no other gods before Him, and in part because, when I met Marcus, I wanted to live my life so I could leave anything behind at any time—easily, like he does—I've woken from that slumber.*

Keiko smiled when Marcus came to the table with the tray of tea. After he sat on the opposite side of the table, he poured them each a cup properly and they exchanged a customary *"Itadakimasu"* ("I will receive") before drinking. They sat in silence for a few minutes, listening to the music, drinking their tea, and Keiko became aware that Marcus shared the silence with her companionably. He'd confided to her that this wasn't something he was able to do easily with others in Japan. Like most Americans, he was largely uncomfortable with lulls in conversations and felt compelled to fill them. *But he's relaxed with me. I sense this as well as I sense that his mind is somewhere else tonight. He's wondering if Dan has responded to his ultimatum, but he's not eager to find out our supervisor's response.*

During his distraction, she glanced across the

table at Marcus, noting that he needed a shave. Haruki could go weeks without shaving, but Marcus needed to shave more than once a day. She wasn't sure why she'd always found his facial hair—along with his strangely abundant chest hair—so compelling, but she did. There was something in-your-face masculine about Marcus, and, though that first day of being with him she'd considered him imposing, she'd come to realize his size and sheer maleness also made her feel safe and protected...even made her feel more *feminine* than any man ever had.

That most of all she couldn't explain. In truth, the whole evaluating-her-own-feelings process was still strange to her. For most of her life, she hadn't considered her own emotions in most situations. She'd grown up in a fairly standard, rigid Japanese home. She did what she was told, what was expected of her, and she didn't question anything. Her first glimpse of the opposite extreme had been in Jordan Palunachek, the daughter of the couple who'd hosted her and Haruki in the foreign exchange program. Jordan had been their age, but she was fiercely independent with a mind of her own and she spoke it at any and every opportunity. Keiko had been stunned by this young woman.

Eventually, the Palunacheks' witness had changed everything for Keiko, as it had for Haruki before her. She knew she'd been transformed from the inside out, but sometimes the radical shift of her viewpoint still left her floundering for guidance. She couldn't discuss the sensation of being lost with her own family—in fact, neither she nor her brother were willing to tell their parents that their *Uchi-Soto* ("we Japanese") mindset had changed. Additionally, they hadn't admitted they'd become Christians—because admitting the truth would be inviting a confrontation that could upset the lives they'd built for themselves. *I would be forced to go home and stay there until the* omiai *is complete. Then I would all but become the possession of my husband in my long-ago-arranged marriage.* To avoid the situation altogether, Keiko hadn't gone home for more than thirteen years. Luckily, her parents considered education second only to familial duty. They never contacted her or Haruki— were never pushy or demanding. They accepted their obligation to the WMMO program and the children's hospital because familial duties had either been fulfilled or could currently wait.

Looking at Marcus, Keiko experienced the troubling sensation that her own grief might overwhelm her. It was true that Dan had asked her to come here, in some part, to "settle Dr. Samuels." The reality was that Marcus had settled her. She couldn't imagine staying in this place if he wasn't here with her physically, on a daily basis. What would it be like to have him become nothing more than a voice at the other end of the phone, or a disembodied presence in an e-mail?

She took a deep breath to loosen the tightness in her chest, but her frustration grew. She felt at a loss to explain her own feelings beyond that Marcus was her best friend. She'd never known anyone like him. Jordan had been a revelation, but something about Marcus was so much wider and deeper and higher than anything else she'd ever experienced. He was kind, thoughtful, generous, equally in the moment as he was in looking to the future. He had the biggest heart she'd ever known. He saw her as a real person, her *own* person...a woman with feelings, a free will, choices, and freedom. No one else, not even Haruki, gave her that kind of respect.

*Respect* is *the right word. Growing up in the West, I see that the Japanese way of respecting is selfish. Others are expected to fulfill required duty and manners to the point of being uncomfortable themselves. That's not respecting someone; it's forcing them to abide by your ideas of right and wrong and giving no thought to anyone else's.* Marcus saw who she was as a person, and he liked her that way—yet he continually encouraged her to be everything she was meant to be, whatever she needed to be. Nothing about this philosophy was the Japanese way. *I'm "me" with Marcus. Letting him go...after all this time? Getting used to living without him? How?*

When he sighed, she came out of her own thoughts to realize that he remained lost in his own, and the tension he was experiencing was palpable. She wondered if her own was to him.

"*Sumimasen* ("excuse me")," she murmured, aware that she was interrupting his thoughts. "Will you miss working and living here, Marcus?"

He looked directly into her eyes—another thing a Japanese person would never do, as it was considered rude. She knew that in the States, the opposite was true. Not meeting someone's eyes when he was talking to you there was disrespectful and shifty. It hadn't been easy for Keiko to re-learn this custom, but she had and she'd marveled frequently at all she would have missed if she hadn't. Gazing into Marcus's eyes equated looking into her own soul in a way she couldn't begin to understand or explain to herself after all this time.

Marcus grinned at her. "I won't miss being called 'san' anything, that's for sure."

His tone was light and kind, teasing, and she

smiled freely. "You think all the etiquette and *aisatsu* traditions here are silly, don't you?"

Even the way he relaxed slightly at her question told her that he trusted her and felt comfortable enough to be honest with her. "Do I think it's silly that, because I prefer cream and sugar in my tea, I'm somehow offending someone? Yeah. I admit it. Why can't I have tea the way I enjoy it? How is that offensive? How does it hurt anyone? Isn't it more offensive to tell someone he has to learn to like bitter, black tea just so he doesn't offend anyone?"

Keiko smiled. His quiet confession was for her ears alone. Warmth spread through her at the certainty. "Yes, but the Japanese won't understand that mentality."

"No. I've seen that. But I haven't relaxed for twelve years for fear of offending someone, even when I can't imagine how I'm doing anything wrong, especially when I'm alone. I would never tell someone else what he or she had to do to be proper. This whole practice feels unnatural and wrong to me. So much of the etiquette stuff I've learned here is the opposite of what I was taught to be polite, proper, respectful behavior. It reminds me of a kind of control kick. If everyone follows it, everyone is under control. But whose control? There's no freedom, no uniqueness, no individuality in a system like that."

"Exactly." The sense of betrayal to her country and family faded almost too quickly for her to wince.

Marcus offered her a ghost of a smile, sharing this understanding privately.

"Tell me about your family's etiquette and traditions," she encouraged. He'd spoken of his parents and siblings so often, she did feel she knew them, especially his mother, but she wanted to hear more anyway. She wasn't sure she'd ever get enough of hearing him talk about his loved ones.

He poured her another cup of tea and she thanked him before he said, "We don't hold to traditions to the point that we can't forgive each other with barely a word if some custom is forgotten or ignored. I guess we're very forgiving and *relaxed*. We're just happy to be together—we don't care to control each other. You can enjoy a person a lot more if you're not trying to get him or her to fit into the hole you've decided they belong in." He shook his head abruptly. "I'm sorry, Keiko. I don't seem to have a filter tonight. I love you and Haruki. I don't have any problems with either of you. Honestly, I don't have trouble with most of the people here. I hope you don't have with me. I guess all this stuff is just building up inside of me."

"Because you're unhappy here," she murmured sympathetically. "It's understandable. You feel you were forced to stay in this country far longer than you ever wanted to."

"Forced, maybe, but mostly I made the choice myself. It's my own fault. And that's not to say I haven't enjoyed so much of my time here. I've gained the kind of fulfillment I could never have known by hiding at home where it's safe and comfortable."

Keiko smiled, and he seemed relieved by her easy acceptance of his words. "What else? Tell me more about your family."

"I think what I miss the most is that every Sunday, after church, my family gets together for a potluck. That's been important to us since my older sister moved out and started her own family. Though we all have separate lives, we're in constant contact with each other..."

He trailed off, and Keiko saw what she could

almost believe were tears in his eyes. She reached across the table for his hand, and he gripped hers tightly between both of his, as if he needed her comfort. The instinct to do so much more...*put my arms around him and hold him close*...was so strong, she almost couldn't fight the urge. "Your family is so close, I can't even imagine. Even when my family all lived in the same house, we had separate lives. I don't talk to my family more than a few times a year. We all accept that. We don't...miss each other, I guess...the way your family does if you don't see or talk to each other often."

He nodded. "Our lives are intertwined. I've missed all that for so long. I've missed so much. My family means everything to me. I feel like I have a hole in my life, inside of *me*. I only hope I can fill it once I'm home."

"You will," she assured him.

He gently let her hands go even when she wouldn't have chosen to separate from him in this way. He inclined his head, agreeing with her assessment, but then he glanced at her again. "Your family... It must get so lonely."

For most of her life, the concept of loneliness had been completely foreign to her. She hadn't grasped that sensation at all until after she'd met Marcus and he'd gone home for a short vacation the first time. She'd already grown attached to their daily interactions and not having him beside her in a physical sense of the word had been excruciating. Since then, she'd arranged all her vacations to coincide with his.

"The Japanese have a very strange idea that never seemed strange to me until I lived in the United States. We're raised with *amae*—dependence. Especially women. Individualism isn't encouraged. Yet we're also raised to be independent to the extreme. *Osekkai!*"

"Mind your own business," Marcus said softly.

"Right. Protect your privacy, follow your dreams, do things your own way at your own pace. In Japan, these two ideas aren't in conflict. They're the ultimate harmony. My parents wanted me to go to a different host family in the exchange program than Haruki because they wanted me to get the maximum experience—a different one, a different education. Get the most out of the learning situation that I could. But if they found out how much I did get out of it..." She shook her head. "...well, that wouldn't be allowed. I would have betrayed everything I am, everything we stand for, even our *ie*—the family system."

Marcus gaped at her in disbelief. "If you can't be free with your own family..."

She quickly squeezed his hand not far from hers on the table, then left off. "You'll be glad to go home, and then you'll have all the things you missed. You'll no longer have a hole in your heart or your life."

"I might have another one," he murmured, running his fingers through impossibly thick, reddish brown hair.

Keiko didn't get a chance to ask him what he meant. He gave a great sigh. "I guess I'd better check my e-mail."

She knew through and through that Marcus had "waffled" according to Dan's wishes because he was open to the idea of God guiding this path He'd put him on. Marcus had spent twelve years serving Christ even when it'd caused him great discomfort and trauma. Yet she understood that Marcus felt he was being disobedient by following his heart now in going home.

When he rose and went to the organization-loaned laptop on the desk, she immediately put her arms around herself, feeling like she might fly apart if she didn't have something to hold her together. If possible, she was as nervous as Marcus obviously was.

## Chapter 2

Marc started to tell Keiko not to bother with the cleanup after their tea in his infinitesimal kitchenette, but he knew if he insisted he'd do it later, she would say the task was no trouble and do it herself anyway. Besides, he knew she was trying to give him privacy...though in an apartment this small that goal was all but impossible. *She wants to find out what's going to happen...and I'm not ready for her to leave yet.*

After turning down the music, Marc sat down at his desk and called up his e-mail program. Free internet, e-mail service and cell phones were part of the WMMO 'package'—a huge perk because it would have been too easy to run up bills of that kind in his endeavor to connect with his family back home. Unfortunately, all services were limited to a certain number of free minutes per month, and, unless there was an emergency, he'd never gone over them. The one thing he'd promised himself when he'd joined the organization was that he wouldn't live extravagantly during his stay here. Japan was one of the most expensive countries in the world, yet he'd managed to get by with a bare minimum of comforts. A missionary would certainly never get rich. Even still, Marc had been able to save a good amount of money during his commission because of his extreme frugality—in part due to his panic disorder that hadn't allowed him to leave the hospital or apartment for any reason except to go to the airport, or, infrequently, ride into the city with Haruki or Keiko for dinner and a musical performance.

He waited for the connection, feeling so antsy, his

leg bounced wildly out of his control. Finally, his e-mail loaded and he immediately saw a letter from his supervisor. He clicked on it, wondering if he'd even be able to understand anything he read. His mind felt so chaotic, he wondered if Jonah had experienced something like this when the Lord had called him to Nineveh and, instead, he'd run in the opposite direction, not seeing, not hearing, not heeding anything but the excruciating desperation inside that compelled him to flee.

After he read the first few lines of Dan's e-mail a half dozen times, Marc frowned, his shock growing.

*I'm sorry to do this via e-mail, Marc, but I didn't feel I was the one to give you this news. Your father insisted that you shouldn't be worried, and so I'm sending this note in lieu of calling your cell phone. There's been an emergency at home. Your mother is ill, but she's not in any immediate danger. I'm arranging your passage home now. It may take several days to get everything lined up. In the meantime, I'm including the phone number and room your mother is in at the hospital in La Crosse...*

Marc's panicked gaze strayed to the bottom of the screen. He saw that Dan was currently online. He clicked the button to instant message him and quickly typed, "What's my mother's condition?"

He sent the sentence. The moments that followed as he waited for a reply were tense and filled with delirious thoughts. First, his supervisor agreed to the conversation, setting the connection in motion, then finally his reply to Marc's question came through: "Stable. She had a heart attack, a mild one, but she is stable and doing well. Her doctor is performing tests and keeping her under supervision."

Marc searched his brain for any past memory of

his mother having heart issues—not that symptoms would mean too much, since twenty-five percent of patients had no symptoms to speak of anyway. He wanted to ask a dozen more questions, but he knew Dan wouldn't have the answers he needed. Before he could begin typing, another message came in with a soft beep: "I knew as soon as you heard about your mother, you would want to go home immediately instead of waiting until the end of the month, as you stated in your previous e-mail."

So Dan had gotten his ultimatum. Marc took a deep breath, then typed, "When I go home, Dan, I'm done. You have to understand that. I've fulfilled my contract twice over. I've been more than patient..." Because he didn't know what else to say, he sat for long seconds staring at what he'd written. Knowing his decision was final and nothing could change his mind now, he sent his message, then waited again. His gaze strayed to Keiko in the kitchen area. Her eyes met his, and he swallowed, aware that his emotional state was naked to her. She always seemed to know just what he was thinking and feeling.

Another message came in, and he looked back at the screen to read, "I understand. I knew that. I accepted last time that I'd gone far beyond the bounds of anyone's patience. And you have had the patience of a saint, Marc. I couldn't ask for more. Your replacement has been trained, and any areas that are left undone can be filled in by the rest of the field staff. There's no reason for you to return to Japan unless you want to or you feel the Lord is calling you back."

Marc's relief was infused with guilt that he stolidly did *not* want to feel. As Dan had stated, he'd gone far beyond what he'd ever considered himself capable of. He'd done everything he could here. Now it was time to leave, time to think about his own life and what *he* wanted to do with it. Wasn't he allowed that choice, the freedom of making a decision that wasn't so much selfish as necessary? He couldn't answer his own question. That area of his conscience was still too tender to allow him to probe too much. He put his fingers on the laptop keyboard again and typed, "I'm done. I'm going home."

Dan's response came in seconds. "All right then. I'll be in contact with your travel arrangements as soon as I can. In the meantime, you might want to call your father to get more details about your mother's condition."

"Thank you, Dan."

When his supervisor left the session, Marc disconnected the IM, then shut down his e-mail program. Standing, he picked up his cell phone from the *kotatsu* table while he walked over to Keiko.

"Is everything all right?" she asked, obviously realizing that something was wrong.

"My mother had a heart attack. She's been hospitalized, but she's stable. Dan's making my travel arrangements to go home ASAP, and he's accepted that I'm not coming back."

Something in Keiko's always calm, serene expression was anything but. He'd never seen her look so lost. She took his hand and Marc squeezed her tiny one, holding it against his heart while he dialed with his other hand. "I'll put it on speakerphone once I get my dad on the line…"

"I don't want to intrude…"

"I want you to know what's going on."

She nodded, leaning against him slightly. He could tell she was relieved with his willingness to share this with her. Later he would ask himself why. Right now his mind was filled with worry for his mother alone.

"What time is it there?" Marc asked her as he waited for the call to connect. He knew Japan was fourteen hours ahead of Wisconsin, but he hadn't looked at the clock since his shift had ended and he'd headed to the dorms.

She glanced at the clock and said, "Nine-thirty in the morning."

A moment later, Marc's father answered the phone.

"Dad, it's Marc. I have Keiko with me. I'd like to put you on speakerphone." When his father didn't object, he did so and held the phone between him and Keiko. "Can you hear me, Dad?"

"I can hear you."

"Why didn't you call me yourself about Mom?"

"I didn't want to worry you, son. Your mother is fine…"

"Dad, a heart attack is serious, even if hers was pronounced mild. When did it happen?"

"A few days ago," his father said.

Marc reeled at the information. Keiko met his eyes, understanding things he knew his father probably wouldn't, even now, after talking with her doctor about his wife's condition over the past several days. "That was too long, Dad. You should have called me the day it happened. Her condition could have rapidly declined, and still could."

"She's doing well, Marcus. Don't worry yourself."

"What has her doctor said? What was the cause of the heart attack? Did she have symptoms before?"

"She never had any symptoms. The doctor says she has something called unstable angina caused by coronary artery disease."

Marc nodded. "All right, Dad. What kinds of tests

are they running on her? EKG, ECG, CT coronary angiogram?"

"I believe one or more of those was mentioned. Dan says you may be able to come home soon?"

Marc had set several deadlines for going home—going home *indefinitely*—but the only people he'd presented them to had been his supervisor and Keiko and Haruki. He hadn't wanted his family to be disappointment if his permanent homecoming hadn't worked out. "As soon as Dan can arrange my flight, Dad, I'm coming home. It won't be longer than a couple of days. And...I'm coming home to stay."

"Your mission is completed?"

"My contract was completed seven years ago. I just stuck around a lot longer than..." *I wanted to. A lot longer than maybe I should have.* "...than expected."

"That's fantastic, Marc. That's just the news that will cheer your mother up."

"I'll let you know when I find out definite flight plans. I want you to call me if anything happens before then, Dad. I'll be calling you, too. Give Mom my love."

"Yes, give Irene my love, too," Keiko said.

"I will."

Marc and his father exchanged love and farewells, then he disconnected. Keiko immediately put her arms around him and hugged him. Marc closed his eyes as he held her small, warm form, drawing in the comfort only she'd given him for so many years in this foreign place. Because he couldn't prevent himself, he prayed out loud for his mother, prayed that he would get back in time and everything would be fine.

Keiko hugged him tighter when the prayer ended and she added her amen. "I'm sorry, Marcus. I hope she'll be all right. I know how much your family means to you."

His emotions were twisted and crazed. He didn't like the thought, *If something happens to Mom I'll never forgive...forgive who? Myself? God? I'm not even sure. All the years I've lost, wasted...* He hated thinking like that, but lately he'd found himself at such a low point in his faith and commitment to missionary work. He wasn't sure who he blamed for his prolonged stay in Japan either. He'd made choices, he'd allowed his supervisor to hedge—he couldn't claim there'd been altruistic or even a thorough Christian motive in his decisions. He could blame no one but himself. But sometimes he couldn't accept that. Sometimes, instead of feeling he'd followed the Lord's will, he couldn't shake the belief that he'd been *forced* into it because he'd never truly had a choice at all.

He eased back to find Keiko smiling slightly. He knew in Japan it was considered inappropriate to express private sadness and so natives smiled when discussing sad things. But he also saw how worried she was about his mother, whom she'd never met but had heard so much about in the years they'd known each other. At times, he'd gotten the impression that Keiko and his mother had communicated with each other frequently—probably via e-mail—but neither would confirm his suspicion. "I'm sorry, Keiko. I'm sorry I unloaded on you earlier. Honestly, I don't have a problem with Japan or the people. Working here has been transforming. And I love you and Haruki and the staff, the patients..."

"Don't apologize to me, Marcus. You never need to apologize to me. You won't allow yourself credit, but you've given every part of yourself to this mission and to everyone around you. You may question your reasons for doing so, but *I* don't. You're a good man. You're a man after God's own heart. No one here doubts that. Dan doesn't. And I certainly don't."

Marc looked into her eyes and one thought filled his entire being. He wouldn't have survived these years without her and her brother. *Without her.* He'd never doubted that the Lord had sent the two Oichi siblings to keep him from going completely insane in this country that wasn't home, was nothing vaguely like the home he loved so much. They'd kept him sane during the times he'd believed he would die if he didn't get back to the States soon.

The thought that he wouldn't have survived without Keiko and Haruki was quickly followed by another. He was leaving. Leaving Japan, yes, but leaving Haruki. Leaving Keiko.

The expression in her sparkling eyes told him what she wouldn't say out loud. Her thoughts paralleled his own. As if by mutual agreement, they drew back from each other, and Marc resisted the urge to put his hands into his pockets, the way he had without censure at home. Of course, in Japan this particular gesture of humility and discomfort was considered rude and could instantly scandalize everyone in the immediate vicinity.

Marc didn't enjoy the strange, sudden unease he felt, and he didn't have to search himself long for the answer to its existence. Long ago, he'd accepted that Keiko wasn't available romantically—Haruki had casually informed him the day she arrived that she was betrothed to another man. Marc had had no choice but to train himself diligently to see her as nothing more than a very close friend. She could never be more to him. His discipline in that regard had been nothing short of excruciating. He couldn't help wondering now if he'd made any headway in keeping their relationship purely platonic. The thought of leaving Keiko, of saying goodbye to her, possibly for a lifetime, made him certain that some part of him was dying a very painful death.

"How long?" she asked, her soft, sweet voice no more than a whisper. "Was Dan specific about your return flight?"

"No. He said a few days. I'll get a chance to say goodbye to everyone. My patients..."

She swallowed with obvious difficulty. "That's good."

Her tone sounded watery, and Marc developed an enormous lump in his throat. "It's getting late. Let me walk you to your dorm."

For once, she didn't insist she'd be fine on her own. She accepted his chivalry. They both slipped back into their shoes and walked quietly to the elevator, then out to the women's dorms in the building next door. He returned her *"oyasumi nasai"* ("good night") a few minutes later and he forced himself to turn away.

*I'm leaving Japan. That's all that matters. Don't think about anything else. This is what I've waited for since the moment the plane landed in this country with me on it the very first time. Before that, I told myself I enjoyed travel—and who wouldn't enjoy a day or overnight trip to Chicago or Minnesota? I'd never been farther than that, so what did I know? I'd never had a panic attack in my life until I got here. I would have happily stayed on the plane, flown back home, and never returned to this country if Haruki hadn't come to retrieve me. I survived...by the skin of my teeth. I fulfilled my five-year contract, and I was ready to leave. Raring to go! But then Keiko came...and I stayed on. Did I stay for her? Even after I knew she was engaged to be married to another man?*

Back in his apartment, Marc closed the door

behind him and removed his shoes. He started to reach for his house slippers but laughed out loud and straightened without putting them on. All these years, he'd worn them even alone just in case someone stopped by. God forbid that anyone should find him in bare feet. He shook his head. *I'm leaving for good, and I'm thrilled. But the thought of never again seeing Haruki…seeing my beloved Keiko most of all…is unimaginable. Because I know I'll never come back to this country once I leave. I know that for a fact. I won't come back for any reason, even for Keiko. Does that bother her as much as it does me?* He didn't want to consider why it would—only pain and disappointment promised in that direction—but he couldn't help it.

    *It's gonna be a long night…and the next few days…endless.*

    Keiko woke with a gasp and sat up, bringing her fingers to her face. She was stunned to realize her cheeks were soaking wet. She gasped again when she realized how crushed her chest felt under the ponderous weight of emotions she couldn't seem to grasp or define. Who was she? What had she become? She'd never been particularly emotional. She'd accepted what was and what had to be, didn't spend all that much time thinking about the ramifications. She'd moved on when there seemed nothing else to do. *But not this time. I can't escape what I know deep inside me, what can't be changed or altered or healed. I have to go with Marcus. I have to be at his side. That's all there is to it. I have to.*

    Strangely, once her decision was made, her chest

felt lighter. This was her only clear, *right* choice. Marcus would need a friend, some support, during the time his mother was in the hospital. He would require aid in adjusting to life in the States again.

Smiling at the role she relished, Keiko caught the last few tears as they strayed down her face. She didn't understand her own mind or this decision she'd made. In whatever way she coated the truth to make it more reasonable, the bottom line was that Marcus meant too much to her to simply let him go and act like her life wasn't in ruins without him. *I don't need to understand the situation any further than that. I just have to do what's necessary to complete the process.*

Rising, she went around the partition to the next room and got her cell phone. It was nearly one-thirty. She wouldn't wake anyone, especially considering the time differential in the West. She dialed Dan's number at WMMO headquarters in Chicago, then sat waiting for him to answer. His secretary fielded the call, asking her to hold. A moment later, Dan greeted her.

Keiko didn't beat around the bush. "I'm sorry to tell you that I'm also resigning, Dan."

"When did you decide this?" he asked.

Instinctively, she analyzed his tone and realized he wasn't surprised by her words. "Just now."

After a pause that made her feel revealed, he said, "You're going with Marcus when he leaves."

*Not a question. Has he been expecting this since he received Marcus's ultimatum? He convinced me five years ago to go to Japan instead of to another WMMO location and admitted outright that he had a missionary doctor already there who would leave the program since his commitment had been up two years previously—and he wanted to prevent that. He thought I could help since my brother and Marcus were already close friends. Whatever his reasons, Marcus stayed on for another full term and then some. Dan believes that has something, perhaps* everything, *to do with me. I'm not sure if that's the case. But I believe it is, too.* "I guess I'm not ready to stop helping Marcus adjust," she offered.

"Are the two of you...*together*?"

Obscene discomfort flooded her at the question Dan had never dared to ask before.

She'd agreed to the *omiai* and the marriage her parents had arranged for her when she was eleven. For that reason, she'd never considered herself free to view any other man as a husband. She'd never seen any man romantically, and until Jordan had married, Keiko had never truly understood what *ren'nai*, passionate love, was about. Her parents had never kissed or shown the slightest affection for each other. Their relationship had been all about 'respect,' a term Keiko no longer fully trusted. She'd strongly suspected that once her younger sister had been born, her parents had ceased to be husband and wife in the intimate sense of the word. Haruki showed his wife little romantic affection—no more than Gin bestowed upon him. In truth, romantic love embarrassed Keiko. She'd always experienced incredible awkwardness even thinking about the ramifications of such a relationship.

"Forget I asked that, Keiko," Dan murmured, obviously as chagrined as she was about the topic. "Suffice it to say, you need me to be looking for your replacement?"

"Yes...but you must understand that I won't be staying around to train him or her. I signed a five-year contract with WMMO, and it was up at the beginning of the year." *And I'm not coming back. I always knew someday I would move back to the States, where I've been a citizen since I began college and haven't allowed my citizenship papers—or even my driver's license—to expire. Of course this means I'll eventually have to tell my parents the truth.* The mere thought sent a chill racing through Keiko's veins.

"I understand, Keiko. The field staff will train your replacement. Do you need me to make travel arrangements for you? I'm not sure I can get the two of you seats together, let alone on the same flight..."

"If you'll let me know Marcus' flight information, I can make my own arrangements. I have a good friend at the Nagasaki airport."

"You're in luck. I just reserved a seat for him on a Monday morning flight out of Nagasaki. The best I could do, I'm afraid."

"I'm sure you did all you could, Dan."

After they hung up, she made a call to a family friend, Sho, who was the Nagasaki airport manager and whom she's always called when Marcus had decided on his biannual vacation days. Sho promised to make all the accommodations necessary to get her on the same flight as Marcus, and in the seat next to him.

With that task in progress, she set down her phone and strode to the window near the desk where she'd set up her tropical fish tank alongside her walking stick insect tank. She would have to find someone to take her pets and her plants. Sasha, her American neighbor across the hall on the dorm floor, would agree. Sasha had often talked about getting a pet but had decided each time not to, since the set-up would require more effort than she cared to expend. *She'll have to be talked into taking care of the stick bug...*

Keiko's mind slid easily to the prospect of leaving the hospital and WMMO as a whole. She experienced no distress in the thought. She'd found fulfillment in her work, but she could be a doctor anywhere. The only home she acknowledged—and had for the past five years—was Marcus himself. She'd realized soon after she'd met him that she belonged with him. She hadn't allowed herself to consider that too deeply. She'd acknowledged the fact and quickly forced herself to focus elsewhere. She didn't know what it meant that she couldn't be without him. Perhaps he would question her actions. Perhaps he would understand. After all, he'd said of his family, "Our lives are intertwined. My family means everything to me. I feel like I have a hole in my life, inside of *me*. I only hope I can fill it once I'm home." She only knew that without Marcus, she was incomplete. Without him, she was empty with gaping holes in her life and in her heart. *Understand? How can he understand what I don't myself?*

Since the one time Marcus had gone home alone for vacation after she'd arrived at the children's hospital, she'd experienced loneliness that had made her come to the decision that her vacation must always coincide with Marcus'. She'd told Dan as much, and he'd since arranged their travel to coincide. She had an apartment and friends in the States. As long as Marcus was only a couple hours from her, she didn't mind not actually *seeing* him at all after their flight home and before their return trip to Japan. In the most vital way, they'd been together, and she'd been satisfied without further consideration. *But I have to think about my feelings now, don't I?*

Keiko sighed and went to make herself a pot of tea. She wished she could ignore the underlying implications of this decision and simply go through with it. If she only had to answer to herself, she would have no problem. But Haruki would be concerned. Marcus would question. *What is there to say? When I ask myself the question why, my only answer...* Keiko swallowed the lump growing in her throat. *Love.*

It was true that she had very little concept of what love was—she'd realized that after she'd accepted Christ. She didn't truly understand friendship. Platonic love. *Ren'nai* was unthinkable. While she'd been a very young child, her mother had been her whole world. But years later, Keiko began questioning if her mother's fondness and care for her had anything to do with her personally. Had she simply been performing her duty as a devoted mother? *Or did things change when she gave birth to Yumako when I was five and her fondness for me diminished in favor of her new, very moldable daughter?*

Only after Keiko saw Jordan's relationship with her parents did she acknowledge that, even within the closest relationship she'd ever experienced with her mother, there'd been a distance...a restraint. No one in her family had ever displayed affection toward her in a physical sense. Yet she'd always felt she was important to them, important most especially to her mother, though she couldn't explain why. Her mother had raised her in the typical Japanese fashion—what Keiko now saw as a contradiction of freedom and unyielding expectation. Even as her parents encouraged her to further her education continuously, she'd forever been aware in the back of her mind that she wanted more out of life than either of them would ever consider for her. The definition of her own dreams had defied her all this time. *Until Marcus. But even realizing how important he is to me, I don't know what any of this means.*

Against her will, she recalled the passionate love she'd witnessed between Jordan and her husband Micah. The two of them couldn't keep their hands off each other. If they weren't kissing, they were holding hands or touching in some very definable way. And when none of those things were possible, they looked at each other with open, naked desire—so much so that the room felt too small and warm to contain their feelings for one another. They spoke to each other in a way that was so intimate, even hearing their words in a one-sided phone conversation had brought Keiko cringing horror...and envy.

*I don't feel mere friendship for Marcus. But do I feel for him what Jordan feels for Micah?* Humiliation made her close her eyes and try to push the question away. It was wrong to imagine what it would be like to be kissed by Marcus, to be held in a way that wasn't platonic or supportive. She was bonded to another, bonded to a man she knew only by reputation. *A bad man I want nothing to do with.*

Keiko sighed, draining the last of the tea from her cup. *Maybe it doesn't matter whether I define any of this. All that matters is that what I feel for Marcus is different from what I feel for anyone else in the world. And the feelings are so strong, they're overwhelming sometimes, especially in light of him leaving...leaving me.*

Yes, she could ignore the ramifications and implications inside of herself, but she knew there would be a flood of questions tomorrow when the news came out that she was resigning. Haruki would be shocked, scandalized. He would demand truths that she wasn't sure she could give. And Marcus would want to know why she was giving up everything...for who? And for what? She wondered if she could tell them what she didn't know herself.

## Chapter 3

It took Marc nearly a half hour to get from his dorm to the cafeteria for breakfast the next morning. Everyone knew he would be leaving in a matter of days—Friday morning, at nine-thirty, in fact. He'd gotten up from a sleepless night, tormented with worry for his mother, superstitious about whether he'd ever truly get home, and sick about leaving the ones he loved here to find Dan's e-mail with his flight details. While his departure date wasn't as soon as Marc had hoped it would be, considering his mother's condition, he was at least glad his siblings had sent him half a half dozen e-mails, assuring him their mother had come through the night in good condition and was doing well.

He just had to get through two more days, which would give him time to say formal goodbyes to everyone. *Goodbye to Keiko. That's the part that keeps tripping me up, that prevented me from even fitful sleep. She's gone with me for years on my trips home. Even if we don't see each other after we part ways at the airport until return flight day, she always feels close enough to be content. But she's not coming with me this time. It'll be so strange not to have her on the plane beside me. I may never see her again. Because there's no way I'll ever come back to Japan. But maybe that's my panic disorder talking. If there was any chance...* Guiltily, he refused to let himself finish the thought.

He finally made it to the table he, Haruki and Keiko shared for nearly all their meals. Japanese breakfast was one of the culture differences Marc hadn't made peace with in twelve years. The mere idea of eating fish, pickles or even rice in the morning repulsed him. Instead of the eggs and bacon, muffins and biscuits, or even cereal he'd grown up with, he'd gotten used to eating fresh fruit alone for the morning meal and he'd come to enjoy it more than he'd ever thought he would. He sat down with his breakfast, and Haruki immediately brought up his imminent departure.

"How is your mother?" Keiko inserted before Marc could respond.

He nodded. "Maintaining. So far, so good. I wish the flight could be today, but I'm just relieved it's soon."

"You'll be back in your element before you know it, Marc-*san*."

Marc grinned at his male friend a little sheepishly. "Maybe the panic attacks will go away permanently."

Having finished his traditional Japanese breakfast, Haruki stood, patting him on the shoulder. "You survived Japan. You're a warrior, brother."

Marc laughed, glancing at Keiko, who was smiling. He noticed she'd barely touched her breakfast. She'd chosen *tamagoyaki*, a rolled omelet that was close to a Western-style breakfast. Its sweetness combined with soy sauce still wasn't quite what Marc could stomach so early in the morning.

"I'm scheduled for an early surgery. *Ohayō gozaimasu* (good morning)."

Nods went all around the table, then Marc turned to Keiko, offering her a smile though he wanted nothing more than to say what he'd been thinking all night: *"You're my best friend, Keiko. I'm over-the-moon-happy about leaving, but I wish you could come with me."*

"I made a decision, Marcus."

"About what?" he asked, surprised because she looked more serious than he expected. As he gazed at her across the small, rectangular table, he realized she appeared as tired as he felt. She'd told him she slept barely four hours a night—it was all she needed, and she'd used that to her advantage while pursuing her education. But she'd never *looked* tired after so little sleep the way she did now. Had she slept at all? Had worry about his mother's condition kept her up? Or something else?

She took a deep breath. "I'm resigning from the organization, Marcus. You know my commitment to WMMO was over at the beginning of this year. I called Dan last night and told him I'm done. That I'm leaving."

Marc could barely fathom was she was saying. She'd said little about her contract ending earlier in the year. When he'd asked her if she wanted to continue with WMMO, she'd shrugged and said she would as long as it made sense to. Now she was telling him... "Your career? You're giving it up, Keiko?"

She shook her head. "No. I'm just resigning from WMMO."

"Do you have an offer to finish your residency somewhere else?"

"No. I just... Marcus, you need a friend right now. You need support..."

Now he was really confused. Why would she go from announcing her resignation to discussing their friendship? What did the two have to do with one another? "I don't understand, Keiko."

She looked down at her barely touched breakfast. "Of course you don't. I'm not making any sense."

"If you don't have another position lined up, what do you plan to do? Why are you leaving now?"

She lifted her gaze, looking more vulnerable than

he'd ever seen her. "I want to go with you, Marcus."

Her face suffused with deep red color, and he couldn't control the embarrassment he felt at the reaction.

"I mean, you need a friend now. Your mother…"

Marc felt punched in the stomach by the implication she was hinting at. She wanted to come home with him. Because he needed a friend. But was that logical? In a sense, she was giving up her career, at least temporarily, and that was a big deal. *A big deal* for a friend.

Still feeling sucker-punched, he couldn't prevent himself from considering things he'd told himself for the past five years were forbidden. Keiko was engaged to another man, a man Marc got the feeling she barely knew. Nevertheless, she was engaged. *Nothing about our relationship is or ever has been romantic. But I can't see any other justification for why she'd give up her career for a friend. Does she feel more for me than she's let on?*

Marc inhaled slowly, shocked because he couldn't deny that the thought of Keiko having romantic feelings for him was far from unappealing. If he hadn't been told by Haruki almost from the moment Keiko arrived that his sister was betrothed, Marc would have pursued her. Nothing could have stopped him except her rejection. "Keiko…I'm going home for good," he said softly.

"I understand that," she murmured, laughing slightly in obvious mortification, glancing away again. "*Gomen nasai.*"

"Don't apologize," Marc said instantly.

When she lifted her gaze to him once more, there was hopefulness in her eyes. "Do you want me to go with you, Marcus? Or maybe I should ask, do you *not* want me to go?"

No denying that he was confused, but he couldn't lie. He lowered his voice. "I would love to have you come with me, Keiko. There's nothing I would like better."

*"I just want to understand* why *you're coming,"* was on the tip of his tongue, but he couldn't get himself to say the words. *Because I don't want to talk her out of going with me. I refuse to do anything to change her mind.*

A large part of his inability to sleep last night had stemmed from the anxiety attack that had gripped him almost as soon as he'd returned to his apartment. He'd felt trapped and suffocated at all the things that could go wrong—first and foremost, that he would lose Keiko forever. Even if they were friends, nothing more romantic, leaving Keiko was a horror to him. He would do it—he would go home and become a daily part of his family's lives again—but he couldn't imagine forgetting Keiko. He wanted *her* to be a daily fixture in his life, as she was here. He would be incomplete without her.

Their eyes locked, and Marc was aware of the multitude of colleagues and hospital visitors around them. This place was way too public for a private conversation. "Can we talk somewhere?"

Without a second of pause, she rose and they walked together quickly toward a vacant meeting room a few hallways over. Once they were inside and silence greeted them, he turned to her. "You said you've already talked to Dan?"

She nodded with that almost desperate, hopeful look on her face again.

"And your friend Sho at the airport?"

Her smile was threadbare. "Sho has already

confirmed my seat next to yours on the same flight Monday morning."

The impulse to demand answers to a hundred questions came and went again, driven away by his fear of making her re-think her decision. He wouldn't ask the questions until it was too late for her to change her mind. Was that selfish? *Maybe it is, but I think it's time for me to find out more about this arranged marriage of hers. Keiko has never wanted to talk about it. Even still, she's made her feelings about the subject clear. She doesn't know, like or want anything to do with the man she's engaged to. I'm not in the least surprised that she only agreed to it because she almost never goes against traditional 'duty' while in the company of Japanese people, and never willfully defies her parents' decisions.*

Gazing at Keiko, Marc wanted desperately to draw her into his arms as easily as he had last night, when she initiated their hug. Their reasons had been acceptable then—his mother's condition. He didn't have a good enough reason now. So instead, he stood a foot from her, unable to deny what he'd tried very hard not to notice in these five years. Keiko was beautiful from the top of her shiny, jet-black head down to her impossibly tiny feet. *Is there any chance that she'll break her promise to marry this other man? Should I even let myself consider she might?*

"Is this all right, Marcus? Having me going with you?"

He swallowed, taking a few steps toward her. He took her hand in his, smiling warmly at her. "The fact that you'd even want to means the world to me. You can't imagine what I was going through..." He shook his head, laughing slightly. She joined him in the soft giddiness, as if they were planning something wonderfully forbidden together. "Let's get together tonight. Can you do that, Keiko? So we can make plans for our trip out on Monday?"

"Yes! Please. I'll make dinner. Your favorites, Marcus. Come at seven-thirty?"

Marc nodded, laughing again, this time in hearty, relieved happiness. Was he imagining that she seemed as overjoyed as he did about this? *Why? I want to know the answer to that as badly as I* don't. *I would be the happiest man in the world if she wanted to become romantically involved with me. But I don't want to let myself fall in love with her only to find out she can't—or won't—break what I know has thus far been a platonic engagement for her.*

While they went separate ways to begin their rounds, Marc recalled one of the strange incidents that had happened to him just after he arrived in Japan. He'd gotten settled in enough that he'd decided to try dating. Surely a romantic relationship would make his time here more interesting, perhaps even enjoyable. But after he'd asked a pretty Japanese nurse to dinner and waited for more than three hours for her to arrive at the restaurant within walking distance of the hospital, Haruki had shown up and patiently explained to Marc the first of many culture clashes. Marc had assumed that because he and the woman had talked about the restaurant, about going there to eat, they would meet there that evening after their shifts, which serendipitously ended at the same time. Haruki had told him that the Japanese didn't do well refusing an invitation—that the nurse had merely been saying to him, "I hope we get along well together in the workplace," with her diplomatic agreement of everything he'd suggested to her earlier that day. For months after that, Marcus had been so embarrassed about his assumptions that he'd gone out of his way to avoid the nurse.

He wondered now if he was assuming too much with Keiko, the way he had with that nurse. *Maybe our friendship means so much to her, she wants to be with me until my mother is better. Maybe she merely wants, as a friend, to help me make the transition of giving up missionary work easier.* Both ideas were plausible—and he hated them. He didn't like feeling this way and realized it wasn't fair of him, but he already knew he'd be devastated if Keiko's intentions didn't mirror his own.

Keiko accepted that it was only a matter of time before her brother found out everything. He'd barely been out of his surgery a half hour before he ran into her making her rounds. As soon as he said, "I called Dan," she understood that he was well aware of the decision she hadn't been sure how to reveal to him. Telling Marcus had been hard enough, but he'd reacted the way she'd hoped. She'd been walking on air the whole morning because the worst had seemed over. She wouldn't be separated from the other half of herself. The pain inside her had healed in anticipation.

Haruki drew her aside to a quiet corner of the ward. Surprising her because they had an unspoken pact to always speak Japanese together when they were amongst other natives, he continued in English, "Marc is going home on Monday. And you're going with him. When were you going to tell me, *imōto*?"

"Soon. What made you call Dan?"

"Because as soon as Marc announced the day and

time of his flight at breakfast, I had the feeling you would do something like this."

"Something like what?"

"Something foolish. You're not just taking a vacation. You resigned, ended your commission. You're going home with him. Why?"

She could have answered a dozen different ways to deflect intrigue from her decision, but Haruki knew her too well. And he'd been in the West longer than she had. While most of her friends and family in Japan wouldn't immediately jump to the obvious conclusion, her brother did and far too quickly. "Have you fallen for him, Keiko?"

"How can you say that? Marcus has always been a perfect gentleman."

Haruki looked at her with a kind of raw scrutiny that made her uncomfortable. "Yes, he has. Because he thinks you're engaged. Maybe only for that reason."

"I don't know what you're talking about. Marcus and I are friends. Just friends. And Ryu has nothing to do with this."

"Doesn't he? You're bonded to the man whether or not he ever sets a wedding date. Does Marc know that?"

"You know he does. You're reading far too much into this, Haruki."

"I'm not sure I am."

"Would that be a problem, even if it was true, although it's not?"

"You're asking if I have a problem with Marc? He's my best friend. I have no problem."

"Don't you?"

"He's not Japanese," Haruki murmured, looking away as if conflicted by his own feelings. "And you're only going to get hurt, Keiko. You have duties.

Responsibilities. Marc isn't a part of those. I don't want you..." He turned back to her and said on a sigh, "...to be hurt."

Keiko shook her head at him. "You've never been an overprotective brother, Haruki. Why are you starting now?"

He just gazed at her, and she knew he didn't believe her protests for a moment. Could her brother understand? She wasn't sure he could. Though he'd become just as Westernized as she had, he'd never left behind what their parents considered the heart of their existence—that all Americans were *gaijin*, outsiders, and to keep the harmony, relationships with them must never be more than skin deep. Beyond that, Haruki took his duty as their family *atotori* or successor very seriously. He didn't believe that accepting Christ had changed anything. Because he was living up to his native traditions despite his conversion, he continued to expect her to do her own duty to family and country.

Keiko had never told anyone about the blackness in her heart. She'd accepted the *omiai* when her parents arranged the introduction of marriage when she was only eleven. But she'd been a different person then. She hadn't known Christ and, at that time, she couldn't have conceived of going against her parents or her culture. The whole concept of marriage when she was that age had seemed far from her—a remote possibility at best. But Ryu, a man much older than her, had become a prominent mogul in Japan with his pornographic manga. He was regarded with the same sex-god awe of the Western equivalent, Hugh Heffner. *And I can't marry him, even if he decides to go forward with the* omiai. *I would rather die than marry a man like him—not simply because he isn't a Christian. But I don't know how I could ever stand against my parents.*

"Are you ready to tell our parents that we're Christians, Keiko? Because that's what you would have to do if you go forward with this in the way I think you're going to."

"With what? I'm just going to the States. I'm a permanent citizen there, you know."

"*I* know, but our parents don't know that either. And I'm not eager to break the news to them all at once, if you know what I mean."

It had been Haruki's idea not to tell their parents about the changes they'd gone through in America. Keiko had gone along with it willingly, if not eagerly. Confrontation had never been her strong suit.

"You gave up your career with WMMO, *imōto.* That's a big deal. And eventually you'll have to tell our family when they find out you're no longer in Japan. What are your plans?"

"Beyond simply *going?*" Keiko glanced away. "I have none."

"What am I supposed to tell them when they ask?"

*Hopefully they won't ask—not for a good long time.* She shook her head. "I don't know, Haruki." That was the whole problem. She didn't know anything except that she had to do this. She hoped the answers would come later, when they were easier to face.

Her brother's expression became resigned. "All right. I'll smooth things over if they ask. But I can't work miracles. If they ask me questions I can't answer, I'll have to direct them to you."

"I wouldn't expect you to do anything else. Thank you, *nii-chan.*"

He shrugged, grinning slightly. "What are big brothers for?"

## Chapter 4

Marc ignored the distinct impression he got that his patient's aunt distrusted him because he was speaking Japanese. Even after twelve years of daily use, he'd never been comfortable with the huge, complex language, but he'd become fluent enough to do his work. The aunt smiled, nodded, her eyes dark and scornful as she said in her own language, "You speak Japanese very well, doctor." The unspoken words, "But that doesn't make you Japanese," would have bothered him far more yesterday. Today, he refused to let anything annoy him. Instead, he inclined his head respectfully, then crouched before Washi. "Are we ready to begin?"

The thirteen-year-old boy nodded. Marc stood and the boy took his hand, motioning to his aunt to remain in the sitting room. Once they were in the treatment room, the two of them fell into their usual pattern since Washi had begun the clinical trial a few months ago. Although most of the patients at the Children's Christian Mission Hospital were chronically ill and had to be hospitalized, their clinical trials also frequently included children whose condition could be maintained from home.

"Is there some reason your aunt brought you today instead of your mother?" Marc asked as he and a WMMO nurse worked together to prep the boy and set up the IV.

"Mother is sad. She believes I am going to die, and Father and Aunt are telling her that I will not reach Nirvana because she has rejected all but the Christian God."

Washi's mother had accepted Christ just after Washi had joined the clinical trial, as had her son, but the persecution she'd received from her husband and sister had kept her waffling between her newborn faith and the unspoken Japanese philosophy that all ways to heaven were good—that having faith in *something*, or many things at the same time, was enough in and of itself. There was no need to concern oneself with details, specific deities and certainly not death. Good karma was all that truly mattered. The bottom line was always that it was better to profess nothing than anything anti-Japanese. Marc acknowledged that the Buddhist belief of attachments hindering 'Nirvana' after death that had been a part of Washi's family's life was the reason the boy's mother now tried to protect herself by separating from her sick child.

"Is she questioning her faith in Christ?" Marc asked, gently inserting a needle into the boy's vein. Washi didn't even wince.

"She believes she can embrace the old and the new."

After directing the nurse in the adjustment of the medicinal flow, Marc glanced at his patient. "What do you believe, Washi-*kun*?"

"I understand this is hard on her. But I believe in Jesus Christ. If I die, I will go to Him."

Of all the Japanese people he'd met in his twelve years, Marc knew very few who "had no other gods before" them. Haruki and especially Keiko were the two strongest Christians he'd met in their faith, but they also had an unshakable reluctance to make waves among their own people. In this country, being ostracized, inviting trouble or conflict, becoming separated from the group collective in any way that put them in an individual spotlight were all situations worse than death for them. Marc considered the whole, unimaginable situation a form of brainwashing—from birth, they were rigorously bombarded with the *Tate Shakai* mentality: Conform. Follow orders without question. The strong controlled the weak and the weak existed to serve the strong. Dislodging a lifetime of engrained beliefs couldn't be easy for anyone.

Swallowing, Marc put a hand on the boy's head affectionately. "You're an inspiration, Washi-*kun*. I'll miss you."

The boy didn't blink. "Your supervisor has agreed to your resignation?"

For the past several months, Marc had been preparing his patients for his departure. He suspected some of them no longer believed he would ever leave, he'd been here so long and he'd so often said that soon he would be going. "I'm leaving on Monday. My mother is ill and I need to go home for her."

"But you will not be coming back?"

"Not this time."

Like most of the other children, Washi showed little reaction to his announcement, but when it was time to leave, the boy wished him good health, long life, happiness and success, as the others had. Marc encouraged him to hold fast to his faith, no matter what happened. Washi assured him he would and that he would be strong for his mother.

Just before lunch, Marc met Haruki and his replacement in a conference room to discuss the morning rounds of their clinical trial. He sensed that Keiko's brother was acting strange and caught up with him after the meeting. "Keiko told you she's going home with me." He'd guessed the reason for his friend's reticence. "It was her decision, Haruki. I want you to know I didn't try to influence her in any way."

"Oh, I know that well enough. I don't blame you at all, Marc-*san*."

*Blame? Does that seem like the wrong word? An inappropriate word for this situation?* "Haruki, can I ask you something?"

If possible, Keiko's brother stiffened more. "Of course."

"I've been here a dozen years, and I guess I still don't understand how betrothals can still be practiced in this country."

"They're not normally, but my family is extremely traditional."

Not comprehending enough to be satisfied, Marc shook his head. "In what way? And try to speak in English."

Haruki grinned, obviously in spite of himself. "All right. The actual agreement was informal. Keiko was eleven. She and her much older bridegroom were brought together by their parents. Our grandmother was matchmaker, and an informal agreement of a future marriage between Keiko and Ryu was reached during the introductory interview. When Ryu is ready, he'll contact our grandmother and the upcoming marriage will be announced and formalized. There's a ceremony between the bride and groom, but the *omiai* will be fulfilled by that time."

Marc had heard the word *omiai* spoken before when it came to Keiko's betrothal. He wanted to know more. "This agreement...you said it's informal. Does that mean less binding?"

"In my family, it is binding. But no, it's not set in stone."

"I don't get it, Haruki."

"In my family, marriages are always arranged. My parents' marriage was. My grandparents'. My own was. In the old days, of course the bride-to-be had little say in the matter, but my parents gave Keiko a choice about whether she wanted to marry Ryu."

"You mean, they gave her a choice when she was eleven years old," Marc said, trying to keep the scorn from his voice. "But Keiko wouldn't go against them at that time, would she? They expected her to agree to the match and she did because *they* wanted it."

Haruki looked at him as if he didn't understand Marc's point. His point was that Keiko had been too young and, in his albeit individualistic view, too brainwashed to fight against what she probably had never wanted for herself in the first place.

"Who is Ryu?"

"His family has a good social background. They're prominent in Japanese society."

Marc didn't comment. He understood the importance of hierarchy in this country. "What do you know specifically about him?"

"He's rich. He'll keep Keiko in luxury."

"But there's something else, isn't there? Something Keiko isn't eager about? Something that makes her hesitant to marry him—beyond the fact that he probably isn't a Christian?"

Haruki nodded but still paused too long. "Ryu is pivotal in the pornography market. Manga and anime. By all accounts, he lives up to his reputation as a *hentai*."

Marc grunted in shock. He'd heard the word used infrequently, but he knew what it meant. *A pervert. A sex pervert. Pornography is so widespread, thriving and accepted in Japan that 'the pink pages' are sold out of vending machines and people read it in public here like we do newspapers in the United States. But...that's not for Keiko. No wonder she doesn't want to talk about her betrothal or consider the fact that the man is her future husband.*

Swallowing, Marc glanced at Haruki. "So she can't get out of this marriage?" he asked softly, feeling like he'd been punched in the stomach.

"If Ryu never calls for the marriage to be made official, she's off the hook. So far, he doesn't seem eager to settle down."

"Does he have any other prospects?"

Haruki frowned. "Do you mean, will he call off the marriage on his own? No. He wouldn't do that. He's made a promise that, if broken, would dishonor his family, Keiko and our family."

"But if she doesn't love him, doesn't want to be with him..." Marc started, his teeth clenching passionately in Keiko's defense.

Surprising him, his friend laughed out loud. "Isn't that an American song, Marc-*san*? What's love got to do with it?"

Marc tensed, bristling at the old-fashioned beliefs. Keiko was free. She was under no obligation but the ones she chose. Chose *now*.

Haruki suddenly grinned. "Did I ever tell you that when Keiko and I were in the foreign exchange program, I fell in love? With someone other than my intended bride."

Marc didn't need to think very hard to guess who'd captured Haruki's attention. "Jordan Palunachek?"

The other man nodded. "She was everything. So different from any other female I'd ever known. So free and outspoken. She didn't have the *kawaii* factor..."

*Cuteness is definitely overrated in this country*

*anyway. And a bit disturbing when a person realizes how 'sexy' old Japanese men find little girls here. Extremely young females are sex symbols in Japan, thanks to the popularity of manga. Thank the Lord Keiko was saved from all that when she came to the United States as a young teenager.*

"Jordan was beyond that," Haruki continued. "She was beyond beautiful. I'd never felt like that before. And I haven't since, though I accepted it when she married Micah."

"But you feel it now, don't you?" Marc said, frowning. "With Gin?"

Sometimes Marc found it hard to believe that this man the same age as him was married and had children with his wife. Haruki saw his family so infrequently and he showed almost no emotion that implied he missed them at all. That was, of course, a Japanese trait, but he didn't talk about any of them much either. Something about that disturbed Marc to the core of his being because he couldn't imagine it. His family meant everything to him. If he had a wife and children, they would be the center of his life.

Haruki shook his head. "Gin and I agreed to the marriage. We have two children and their future is the most important thing to both of us."

When his friend did deign to continue, Marc blinked at him in shock. "What are you saying? Your marriage is over? You don't love your wife anymore, if you ever did?"

"Why does that surprise you, Marc-*san*? Our marriage was arranged. She's become a relative. A mother now. She doesn't have any interest in being anything else anymore."

Marc tried to make excuses in his mind for what Haruki was implying. He couldn't mean that his wife had become a mother and ceased to be a beloved wife. That was illogical, senseless, even self-defeating. "If there is no love in marriage and the couple no longer sees each other as sexually viable after the wife has children...how do you..." Marc flushed and looked away but couldn't get himself to back down from asking the question. "Well, how do you get your romantic and sexual needs met?"

Haruki shrugged. "Most Japanese men? With pornography, talking to, watching, groping a pretty girl... Those things satisfy desire. You might have heard that a Japanese man's testosterone level is lower than a white or black man's. Not me, of course."

Marc tried to be relieved at hearing that, but all he could feel was utter horror—because he'd seen all the evidence of what Haruki was saying. Japanese society was based on being sexually satisfied in these ways instead of...*instead of the American version of morality. Sex and love are tied integrally. Fidelity and a good sexual relationship with a spouse are critically important to well-being.*

"I'm a Christian, Marc-*san*. My ideals have changed radically, but my wife would be shocked if I approached her that way now. She expects me to have affairs if I have sexual needs that aren't being satisfied. If she needs to..."

"No. I can't accept that. Call it narrow-minded..."

"We're from two different worlds, Marc-*san*. I've crossed into yours and I understand your view the way few other Japanese can. But you have romantic ideals that I'm not certain I can accept. We can understand each other without agreeing, *ne ka*?"

Marc couldn't speak. His entire being was wrapped up in the question of whether Keiko shared her brother's views. *Please God, no...*

"You will marry when you finally get home?" Haruki said, more of an observation than a question.

In the past, Haruki would have been friendly in a teasing way that Marc expected yet didn't get this time. Something about his friend's words sounded hard, uncertain, even unfriendly. "Marriage is the ideal for me. It has been all my life. I never expected to be forty years old and still unmarried, without children."

"You'll make it a priority now?"

What could Marc say? Even if his friend was sending him an unspoken warning about having anything beyond friendship feelings for his sister, he couldn't lie. "Yes."

"And you'll have children as soon as possible after you're married?"

"If my wife likes the idea."

"And after she becomes a mother?"

Marc swallowed the sensation of being threatened by a man who'd been his lifeline since arriving here. "When I get married, my passion for my wife will be romantic and sexual until the day one of us dies. Anything else is unimaginable to me. After Christ, my marriage will be the priority in my life, even above children, though our family will be central to both of us."

"You already know this?"

"Yes. I already know this. My wife and our family will be my *life*."

As he and Haruki parted, Marc wasn't certain if he'd reassured his friend...or, after all this time, given him grounds to see him as an enemy. He couldn't understand how Haruki would prefer that his sister marry a godless *hentai* who would eventually betray and dishonor their marriage vows over a Christian man who would treat her with the respect and lifelong adoration she deserved. *Worlds truly collide here, especially for those who attempt to give their lives to the Japanese heritage* and *to Christ. In so many ways, it doesn't seem possible to me to divide loyalties like this because both require absolute adherence.*

Something had to give, and Marc could see the clash would come soon. He just prayed he wouldn't be on the opposite side of Haruki, but most especially *Keiko*, when the hammer fell.

Keiko realized the extent of the rumors when the fifth nurse she encountered on her morning rounds asked if something was going on between her and Dr. Samuels. The Japanese girls were alarmed, even scandalized, the Americans intrigued. Her neighbor in the dorm, Sasha, was all smiles. "He's gorgeous, isn't he? I've always thought so. I've got a thing for big, muscular, dark men with adorable dimples like that. But then I'm spoken for." Sasha's new husband was slightly younger than her and still working on his education in the States before he entered the WMMO program. "I thought you and Dr. Samuels were just friends. And you're engaged, aren't you? Didn't you tell me that when I first got here?"

"My commitment to the program has been fulfilled," Keiko said, feeling increasingly upset as she tried to focus on the chart she was updating. She'd never considered that everyone would find out about her resignation—especially this fast. She didn't expect to have to explain her actions to anyone but Marcus and her brother. Every single person who'd questioned her about her plans assumed that she and

Marcus were a couple—that they'd been keeping their relationship a secret all this time. *Why do they assume I'm doing this because Marcus and I are in love?* The thought made her uncomfortable to the extreme, and she couldn't decide why. Everywhere her mind went to dissect her reasoning left her more embarrassed and uncertain.

"Yeah. Your commitment was over at the beginning of the year," Sasha said, walking beside her out of the patient's room. "But you never said you were resigning, especially at the same time Dr. Samuels was. I didn't even know his resignation was for sure until today. Is it just a coincidence that the two of you are leaving together? To go to the States?"

*Is Marcus putting up with this stuff from our colleagues?* "I'm an American citizen."

Sasha gave her a friendly grin that made Keiko feel exposed. "It's not a crime to fall in love, Keiko. And who could blame you? He's a total hunk. And he's just *good.*"

*"But I'm engaged"* came to Keiko's mind as a defense, but she couldn't get herself to use the excuse. She knew the only way to get through this minefield was to ignore the gossip as much as possible. She and Marcus would be leaving on Monday. They wouldn't have to put up with the rumor mongers much longer.

She changed the subject by asking if Sasha would mind taking her pets—including the walking stick. The other woman grimaced at her, but Keiko rushed to assure her, "It's really no trouble. Just keep a stick in the tank for the insect to climb on, make sure you maintain the slight humidity and keep the sponge damp. It eats romaine lettuce or apple leaves. It really doesn't require much care."

"Okay. But it's creepy."

Keiko was used to people thinking her choice of pets were strange. She'd never outgrown the fascination with them after raising a profusion of varieties as a child. Marcus was the only one who said he thought her hobby was "cool." He'd told her he also kept insects when he was younger.

"I hope you don't mind," Sasha continued, "but I was also thinking about requesting your apartment— then we wouldn't have to move your pets. I love the way you set up all your panels to divide the rooms...though truthfully, there isn't much *to* divide."

Keiko agreed, and she and Sasha parted. More than anything, she hoped she hadn't caused Marcus embarrassment or stress over her decision. He'd seemed so... *So happy. So relieved!* The warm feeling she'd gotten at his reaction earlier flooded her again. Somehow, that memory got her through the remaining hours of her shift.

As soon as the final staff meeting concluded, she rushed out to get groceries. Back in her apartment, she started the rice, then she cut and seasoned the beef, wrapped it and put it in the fridge. The meat just had enough time to become tender and flavorful before she cooked it. Next, she prepared the vegetables. Marcus didn't like fish of any kind, and that made cooking for him difficult, since fish was a staple in Japanese cuisine and one she'd grown up enjoying. One of the few Japanese dishes he enjoyed was *Gyundon*, a beef *donburi* bowl. He'd enjoyed it for the first time at a restaurant they'd gone to after attending a concert in Osaka. He'd claimed on many occasions since that hers was the best he'd ever tasted. She'd also picked up a baked type *Wagashi* confection, since Marcus' favorite course in any meal was dessert.

Once she finished her preparations, she glanced at

the clock. She had time to shower and change before he arrived. She'd barely finished her shower when she heard her phone buzzing. Quickly, she reached for it on the counter in the tiny cubicle bathroom. For a moment, she worried it was Marcus—worried his mother had taken a turn for the worse, worried that he wouldn't want to come to dinner. But it was only Sho, confirming her earlier "solid hope" that her flight plans could be meshed with Dr. Samuels' on Monday. She thanked her friend profusely, then ducked back into the shower and finished washing quickly.

Tomorrow, she and Marcus would both be packing to leave. She'd called Jordan during her lunch break today, and she and Micah were excited about having her stay with them. The couple lived in La Crosse, Wisconsin, with their newborn baby. La Crosse wasn't far from where most of Marcus' family lived in Peaceful.

"I'm staying with my father at the house, like usual," he told her a half hour later when he arrived, cleaned up and smelling good enough to eat. "I'm really glad you decided to stay close instead of going to your apartment in Chicago."

He looked much more relaxed than she'd expected him to. *Maybe no one confronted him about my decision to go with him, to resign.*

Her thought was quickly refuted with his sheepish grin. "You wouldn't believe how many people asked me today why you're going home with me."

"Oh, Marcus, I'm so sorry. I was hoping you wouldn't have to face what I did during my shift."

"You, too?"

She nodded. "Relentlessly."

He laughed out loud, and the deep sound reverberated inside her chest and made her feel glorious. How did he always manage that?

"In any case, I am sorry you got dragged into the gossip."

He shrugged. "Actually, that part didn't bother me so much."

"Something else did?" she asked anxiously.

"Haruki."

His tone was soft and realization flooded her. "He didn't confront you, did he? He acted so strangely with me when he found out today. Dan must have called our manager here at the hospital to let him know our plans, and everyone learned from there. I've never seen Haruki go 'protective brother' before. I don't understand it."

"Don't you?" Marcus questioned, his tone impossibly softer yet reaching the intended target.

"What do you think?"

"I think that your brother struggles against the *Uchi-Soto* mind-set that nearly everyone I've met here has."

*Us and Them.* Keiko nodded her complete agreement.

Marcus conceded. "It's harder because he's a Christian."

"That's true. Some part of him believes I'm betraying our culture, our family, our way of life. He's also afraid our parents will learn that we're Christians. Neither of us wanted to make waves by admitting the truth to them. It would change everything."

His dark eyes were strangely conflicted and contemplative as Marcus looked at her. Finally he said, "I got the feeling it was more than that, Keiko. I got the feeling it had more to do with your fiancé."

Keiko started at his use of that word.

"Haruki told me some things about him. I can

understand why you wouldn't want to marry him,
Keiko. Why do you have to?"

She turned away from him, quiet for a moment,
then rose and went to the kitchen to start dinner.
Marcus followed her. They'd cooked together many
times, and they both moved to tasks as if they'd been
previously designated.

"It's hard to explain, Marcus."

"I know. I understand how deeply ingrained
tradition and duty is in your culture."

"Then you know my only real hope is that Ryu will
never want to marry me."

"You're a Christian now. You're not obligated to
fulfill a promise you made when ultimately it wasn't
your choice."

Keiko couldn't help smiling slightly at that. After
twelve years in this country, he truly didn't
understand the Japanese way. She shrugged. "I've
heard he's ill."

"Really? What kind of illness?"

She glanced at him. "Black Syphilis."

Marcus' entire face changed with his disbelief.
"You're not serious, Keiko. Wasn't that a made-up STD
used to frighten GI's away from the prostitutes in
Korea after World War II?"

"Maybe. But I can't help wishing it was real." If Ryu
really had an incurable sexually transmitted disease...
*Either he dies of it before we marry and I'm off the hook.
Or he agrees to marry me and infects me. Dear Lord,
don't let that happen!*

"Are you...you and Haruki...*afraid* of your parents?
Do you think they'll...what? *Disown* the two of you if
you admit you're Christians?"

"Something like that," she murmured.

"But what specifically will they do?"

"I think they'll force me to go home and live there until Ryu contacts Grandmother, saying he's ready to fulfill the *omiai*."

Marcus put his hand on her arm and gently turned her toward him. "*Force* you? You're an adult, Keiko."

"I know...I... You just don't know my parents."

He stood only inches away from her, touching her in a way that made her wonder if he was fighting to pull her closer to him. His expression was so strange, so foreign. Yet...didn't she know that expression?

"I know I don't understand so much about this country and its culture and customs, Keiko, but... If you felt you did have a choice about marrying this man Ryu... If you chose not to, what kind of man would you date?"

Heat flooded into her face. "I've never dated anyone, Marcus. I've never even thought about it. I couldn't."

"Because of the *omiai*?"

"Yes." *But I'm a Christian now, and if I had the freedom, if he wanted the same, I would want to date a man like Marcus. A wonderful Christian, a hunk, a man who's just* good. Keiko felt her cheeks warm.

As if they were both embarrassed about the direction of this conversation, they turned back to preparing the meal. She tried to think of something to say and finally decided on, "What about you? Your family is the most important thing in the world to you. They must all wonder why you don't have a family of your own by now. Is that something you'll consider when you get back to the States for good?"

"I've wanted to fall in love, get married and start a family for as long as I can remember. The Lord kept saying 'Wait. Wait for My timing.' Once my mother is well again, it'll be my top priority. I'm not willing to wait any longer."

"So...you have someone in mind?"

Surprising her, Marcus laughed out loud. "Not exactly."

*What does that mean?* Keiko couldn't guess, and he didn't ease her suddenly troubled mind on the subject. Certainly not when he asked, "Keiko...I don't want you to change your mind about coming home with me— not at all. You can't imagine how right and perfect it felt to me when you told me your decision to resign from WMMO. But I can't help wondering *why* you made your decision."

Keiko sighed, unable to look at him. She couldn't answer him. She didn't even know the truth herself. "I'm not unhappy with my career. But...ever since I went to the States to live with the Palunacheks, I've known where my home is. I became a United States citizen for that reason, and I want to return there and live in your country for the rest of my life."

"Does your family know you became an American citizen while you were in college?"

"No."

"You and Haruki have a lot to tell them." His tone sounded slightly shocked.

Yes, they did. But she wanted to wait. As long as she possibly could, she wanted to wait to disclose any unexpected reality to her family. For once, she could explain her logic on that count. She wanted to wait until she felt in control of her own life. Even at the age of thirty-three, she considered herself subject to her parents' wishes and expectations. She had no idea how to shake the sense of obligation. It'd simply been easier to follow Haruki's advice in not telling them *anything*...and staying away from home, possibly indefinitely. Yet she accepted that Marcus' concerns were valid. One way or another, sooner or later, the truth would come out. How could she be strong enough to stand firm against the inevitable storm that would sweep through her life then?

## Chapter 5

Haruki had troubled himself to take an hour off Monday morning to see them to the airport. He warned them to be safe in their travels, to take care of their belongings, not to worry because nothing could go wrong, and nothing would be stolen. Marc couldn't help feeling that the well-wishing was more than a little forced. He got the impression his friend was going against his deeply ingrained instincts to act as if everything was hunky-dory, all remained the same.

Before they'd gone to Keiko's apartment that morning, Marc had attempted to assure her brother that there was nothing going on between the two of them, but he knew Haruki didn't buy it. *Does he know something I don't? Did she say something to him? More than she's said to me since she announced she was going with me? I can accept that she fell in love with America and wants to live out her life there. I can even buy that that's why she resigned. But why* now*? Why not at the beginning of the year when her contract expired?*

Marc had gone out of his way during the past weekend not to say or do anything that might make Keiko change her mind about leaving Japan with him. He didn't think he could bear the devastation if she decided not to go through with it. His worry about whether her plans would alter and other silly superstitions he couldn't seem to rein in before they became full-blown had made him live in fear. He imagined himself once more as Jonah, closing his eyes and ears as he ran in the opposite direction the Lord was commanding him to go.

Even sitting on the full plane with Keiko next to

him, all directions pointing homeward, he wasn't convinced what he wanted would happen. Ultimately, he couldn't shake the belief that he'd given over a good portion of his life—possibly his *best* years—to God's will. His regrets were few but he had to confess that he harbored one or two that would remain with him for life. He'd accomplished something, he was proud of his work. He'd given up a tremendous amount, too— willingly.

When was it his turn to live his life the way he'd longed to? He'd fulfilled spiritual career goals he might not have chosen a second time if he'd been given the chance to revise them. But he'd ignored his own need for a lover and companion for life, a family. Surely asking to have a chance at an emotional, romantic and sexual relationship wasn't too much. He was forty years old, after all. More than anything in the world, he wanted a wife and children, and he wanted to be young enough to enjoy them. An oversized portion of him expected God to refuse to let him go, just as Dan had for so long.

*Am I rebelling against the Lord now? By leaving? Because I can't be swayed. I'm going. That's all she wrote. The only thing that can stop me at this point is divine intervention. I don't know what's right or wrong. I can't help thinking I don't even care about that anymore. God help me!*

His breathing was becoming erratic and ragged, his chest tight with the dread that something would prevent this flight from taking off and making it all the way to the United States—that in fact, he'd never be able to leave Japan for as long as he lived...

Two small hands covered and enclosed his as much as possible. Marc glanced up from his shaking limbs to see Keiko smiling reassuringly next to him.

His mind whirled as if he'd been spinning in endless circles for the last several minutes. Something about her tender touch and the sight of her comforting expression grounded him. Abruptly, he felt his world set down on a stable plane once more.

"How is your mother? Have you heard anything this morning?" Keiko asked.

He nodded. "She's good." With his face still turned to hers, he laid his head back on the seat and closed his eyes.

"You'll see her soon."

"And we'll relive the same day all over again once we're home."

She chuckled softly, and Marc realized she was close enough to kiss. He could have at that moment. Easily. Gratefully. With his whole heart. He'd been seconds from a panic attack, and she'd staved it off with her calming presence. He closed his eyes again.

"You're glad to be leaving Japan for good," she murmured so no one else could hear.

Marc looked at her and found her face mere inches from his now. She was dressed casually yet elegantly in designer jeans and a silky top. Her hair was in an absolutely adorable ponytail, her long bangs framing her small, beautiful face. "I'm glad you're with me, Keiko. I don't think I could get through this without you."

"I'm glad."

He laughed out loud, trying to sound scolding. "You're *glad*?"

Her content, happy expression didn't alter. "I'm glad to be with you."

He nodded, inevitably wishing things could be different. That she wasn't engaged to a pervert her family, unbelievably, approved of, that she was free.

*There's no one else I'd rather be with than this woman. But I can't. We can't. But I'm not ready to accept that.*

Pushing away disappointment or dragging emotions, he sighed. He was going home. With the woman he couldn't imagine living without. Nothing else mattered. "The more I think about it, the more I realize that my feelings about Japan have been misplaced in a lot of ways." He spoke softly, for Keiko's ears only.

"What do you mean?"

"I mean, if Dan had sent me anywhere else—the Bahamas, Italy, the Soviet Union, Ethiopia, the moon...it wouldn't have mattered. None of them are home to me, could never be, so I would have had the same reaction. When all is said and done, I am grateful he chose Japan. I probably wouldn't have met you or Haruki anywhere else. I got to work with people and patients who changed my life at the children's hospital. The Lord used me, and I'm grateful. I'm blessed."

Keiko smiled in return as if his words blessed her. "I feel the same way. And you're right that you wouldn't have met me anywhere else."

"What do you mean?"

"I suppose I can tell you this now and hope you won't take it the wrong way."

Marc tensed slightly. "Tell me what?"

"Five years ago, Dan knew you were going to leave. Your contract was up, and Haruki had confided in him how restless you were becoming at the prospect of going home. Dan asked me to come here when my contract started. He was hoping I would "ground" you. I agreed mostly because Haruki was in Nagasaki. He'd already told me all about you, but it wasn't until I met you that I understood why my brother thought the world of you. I also understood then why Dan was so reluctant to let you go. You're exactly the kind of doctor and witness for Christ that WMMO looks for. Once I met you myself, my reasons for staying were all about you. You've blessed my life just by being in it. Dan did *me* the favor, asking me to come to this mission site."

Marc should have been upset at the revelation, but how could he be? Dan had brought Keiko into his life on purpose. "I always wondered if Dan had something to do with your appearance, though I couldn't imagine specifically how he was involved."

"Are you angry?"

"At you? Never. But you're right. I did stay even after my contract expired because you came. Those two years I stayed after my contract expired had everything to do with Dan and Haruki throwing things at me that I felt I couldn't refuse. If you hadn't come along when you did, I would have left for sure soon after that. I have to admit that, deep down, I do feel manipulated by Dan. If my mother hadn't gotten ill, I expect he would have hedged forever and tried to get his way."

"You wouldn't have put up with it."

"I'd like to think I would have stuck to my ultimatum, but he talked me out of my decision to leave more times than I can count. Maybe he didn't intend to, but he made me feel like I would be going against God Himself if I refused to stay."

"Do you still believe that?"

"Yes. I live in fear that He'll stop this. That the plane will crash..."

"The Lord isn't out to get you, Marcus. We'll get home. I promise you."

"You don't think I'm running away?"

"Running from what? You've given your life to medical missions. You'll continue to do so—from home. I don't doubt that for a second."

Marc didn't feel nearly so sure.

The pilot came on the intercom to announce their take-off. Marc prepared his mind and body for the imminent trauma he experienced each time a plane took off and set down. As usual, Keiko held his hand and helped him through it.

"Tell me about your parents," he murmured when the plane was airborne and he could catch his breath again.

"I've never really known my father well. He simply wasn't a large part of my life the way my mother and grandmother were. He worked most of the hours of the day and came home after I was in bed for the night. He was always gone when I got up in the morning. When he was there... Well, I never dared to defy or disappointment him. He held great authority over all of us. But he deferred to my mother and grandmother in almost everything in our household except spiritual matters.

"We have a shrine in our home, and my father went there at least once a day. He talked to us about those things when he was around—about many aspects of various religions, but little made sense to me. After I became a Christian, I realized the things he believed in spiritually had made him superstitious. While it's normal in Japan for everyone to believe in syncretism, accepting and practicing many faiths, most don't really take anything spiritual seriously. Religion doesn't affect day-to-day lives and decisions. But my father was different in that regard. Strangely, he was very afraid of the afterlife and deities in general, and tried to make sure we were always living aware of our karmas. He was superstitious to the point where he would allow his fears and what he referred to as visions influence our household and his business decisions."

"Keiko?"

She glanced up at him, her eyes far away.

"Are you aware that you're speaking of your father as if he was a part of your past instead of your present? As if he's no longer alive?"

She seemed startled at his gentle words. "I…I guess I just haven't seen him since I was a young girl. Just as you say, it almost seems like he's no longer a part of my life."

"So you were closer to your mother?"

She nodded. "My mother and grandmother were my entire life as I was growing up, until I was five years old. They made me their entire life until my sister Yumako was born, just as Haruki had been their center before me. Japanese mothers give everything for their children. Yumako seemed needier than I ever was, so maybe she required all my mother's and grandmother's attention. I never really got to know my sister, and Yumako didn't make it easy. She just had no time for me—mainly because we had so little in common. But I feel such a strong responsibility toward her. I can't even explain it.

"Anyway, it wasn't until Yumako was out of school and had a job that my mother went back to working with my father, but she's still pivotal in my sister's life. If I'd never gone to the United States and seen how American families live, how the Palunacheks were with Jordan, I might never have realized that I didn't really understand what a family could be. Even when Jordan lived at home and followed her parents' rules, she was free. No one tried to control her mind or tell her what her duty was, what she should believe. She wasn't made to feel like she was being disloyal to her family, to her entire culture, if she made a choice her parents might not approve of. Not once in my entire life until that point did I understand I could be my own person and make my own choices. That I could be accepted and appreciated for who I was. In Japan, everything is done for the 'benefit' of the family, the group, the country. You contribute to the whole, which can be admirable, but there's no such thing as the individual. Ever. Individuals aren't valued—they're ostracized and belittled.

"I began to see that my mother's and grandmother's love and doting on me had been done for a specific purpose—to get me to feel obligated to their values, their decisions, the duties that they expected of me. If I went against any part of that, I would be an outsider. Suddenly, love no longer felt like love because it was conditional. The love they gave expected me to be a mindless robot, just going along with my duty. I don't know that any other person would feel like I did, but realizing all that devastated me. I felt so lost, wondering if my mother really loved and cared for me. The fact that she doesn't contact me, that she waits for me to contact her...while it's expected, I often wonder if it's because she simply doesn't care."

"Is that part of the reason you don't want to tell your parents the truth about you and Haruki accepting Christ, about your United States citizenship?" Marc guessed.

"Yes. I worry that they'll reject us. I'm not ready to lose my family, even if I no longer feel assured of their genuine love for me."

Marc squeezed her hands tenderly. "I can't

imagine what you've gone through, Keiko. It makes sense that you're wary to lose so much."

"Thank you. For listening. For understanding."

"It's the least I can do. You're always there for me."

She smiled, and Marc basked in the glow of her companionship. "So…what are your plans once we get in?" he asked.

"I hope you don't mind, but I'd like to go with you to see your mother at the hospital."

A tightness in his chest he hadn't been consciously aware of eased at her words. "Mind? It would mean a lot to me. My brother Josh and his wife are dropping off the old family car in the short-term parking lot at the airport so we can use that. I have the keys from previous visits. I'll take you to Jordan's when we're done at the hospital."

She shook her head. "I kept my driver's license renewed. I can get a rental…"

"I insist. I've kept my license permit up-to-date, too."

"You'll be staying with your father?"

"Until I get my own place. I'm hoping to take a couple months off, just to enjoy life again, before I think about what to do with my career."

"That sounds like a great plan. You shouldn't have any trouble doing that, right?"

"No. I've managed to save a great deal these past twelve years. And I still have all the furniture from the apartment I shared with a friend while I was in college and medical school. It's in storage, so I won't have to take out much money to furnish my own place." He liked the idea of buying a house, his first house, in preparation for a family. But that would probably have to wait. When he got home, his first priority would be to make sure his mother pulled through her illness.

"Did you sleep at all last night?" Keiko asked.

He raised an eyebrow. "I don't think I've slept since all this was decided." Once their flight got in, his jet lag probably wouldn't hit immediately. When it did, he knew from experience he would crash for fourteen hours straight.

Keiko had never been sure what to think about things that were seemingly "meant to be", but each time she arrived in the United States and deboarded a plane, she recalled the fact that Jordan Palunachek was the best friend of Marcus' youngest sister. Somehow it seemed odd to her that Marcus should know the people who'd been so pivotal in her transformation. He might be surprised to learn himself that she and his mother had been conversing via e-mail since the first time Marcus had introduced them during a phone call in Japan. She'd never actually met anyone in his family in person, although his mother had been trying to arrange it for years. Until Marcus asked her to accompany him to meet his family, she hadn't felt the introduction was appropriate. She'd longed for it terribly, and today finally she would get her wish.

They processed through all the usual airport customs, then went to retrieve their luggage and get the car that had been left for them by one of his brothers.

She glanced across the leather seat at him. "See, God isn't out to get you," she teased.

He faced her with a grin. "Maybe not. Or maybe He'll wait until later." The twitch of his eyebrow and lips made it obvious he was being facetious.

"Do you really believe that, Marcus? That the Lord wants you to serve Him and have nothing at all for yourself?"

"You see it all over in the Bible—Jonah, Paul. Neither of them had a choice. Their ministries were their whole lives. Did they have wives, children? Doubtful."

"Of course they had a choice—although Jonah may have done what was right just to get it over with, not really to be obedient or kind to those who needed his message. That's certainly not you. You must see in reading that book in the Bible that, even when Jonah tried to rebel and run away, the Lord continued to work His will through him. He brought Jonah where he needed to be."

"And that's what I think He did with me. But I'm judgmental, just like Jonah was. You can't deny that."

"Maybe. Not really. If you are a teeny-tiny bit, it's your only fault."

Marcus laughed with disbelieving relish, and Keiko smiled contently. He reached over and squeezed her hand. "What would I do without you, Keiko?"

*Let's never find out.*

"I'm home. Thank the Lord. And I've got you beside me. Soon I'll see my family. I'm the happiest man in the world at this moment, Keiko. The only thing that could improve this bliss is my mother making a full recovery."

Even as hopeful and truly joyful as Keiko also felt, she hadn't been able to shake the conversation they'd had Saturday night in her apartment. *"I've wanted to fall in love, get married and start a family for as long as I can remember. The Lord kept saying "Wait. Wait for my timing." Once my mother is well again, it'll be my top priority when I'm home. I'm not willing to wait any longer."* Maybe Marcus didn't have anyone in mind at the moment, but she knew that by any and all American standards, Marcus was highly attractive to a majority of women. It wouldn't be long before every eligible bachelorette in the surrounding area was alerted to the fact that he was available. They would come running in droves. *What will I do then? Our friendship will have to change to accommodate his girlfriend...or wife. Then does it matter that our friendship sometimes seems meant to be, even to me—a wary disciple in the area of 'fate' and romantic love?*

"Seems so strange that I've never met your family before," Keiko murmured when they arrived at the hospital and he searched for a parking space. She considered adding that his mother had e-mailed her several times a week for many years. In ways, Keiko felt she knew the woman better than her own mother because of their frequent communications back and forth. *Irene Samuels has helped me love her son. Did she plan that? She talks about him like he's a saint, her favorite child, but I suspect that if any woman can love all her children equally, in the amounts each one needs, it's her. I bet all her children feel like the most special person in her world. She makes me feel undeniably special to her. She makes me feel like I belong with Marcus.*

"It does seem strange you haven't met any of my relatives before, doesn't it? Judging by the number of times I've talked about you and Haruki, I bet they feel like they do know you though."

"And I feel like I know them after all the times you've talked about them." With shock, Keiko realized she felt nervous about meeting them. What would or did they think about her? Had Marcus told them—told his mother—she was engaged to another man? She'd never considered that. *But why would he tell anyone? So they wouldn't jump to the conclusion that he has any romantic interest in me? If he hasn't mentioned it...* She pushed the thought away. She couldn't let herself wish for things that weren't possible. Already she suspected the pain of loss where Marcus Samuels was concerned would be more difficult than anything she'd dealt with in her life thus far.

"When I called from the airport, Dad said everyone took time off to be at the hospital."

"To greet you?"

The expression on his face was a combination of humbled awe, and Keiko felt almost relieved when he hugged her from the side, his arm around her shoulders, as they made their way into the bustling hospital. In moments, they were in an elevator, riding it up to the floor his mother was staying on. Marcus had just disentangled himself from her when the doors slid open and faces that looked similar to his own came into view. She knew without a doubt both men standing near the bank of elevators were his brothers and the woman was his sister—they all had those irresistible dimples and the almost obscene good looks. Besides, she'd seen countless photographs he kept in his cell phone and other electronic devices of most of his family members.

The siblings greeted their brother effusively, as if he was a long-lost relative. Keiko got tears in her eyes as she eased away to give them a bit of privacy. Yet she didn't get far. Marcus drew her back to him and introduced her by her first name. She could tell she was familiar to them by the way they welcomed her with warm, loving hugs and friendly words.

"We've kind of taken over the waiting room," Tamara told them.

Until they arrived at the overflowing room, Keiko wasn't sure what she meant. She gaped at Marcus. "These are all part of your family?"

He nodded, chuckling at her astonishment. The next fifteen minutes were more of the same affectionate greetings from his brothers and sisters, brothers- and sisters-in-law, and all their children and children's children. Realizing that every one of them assumed that she and Marcus were more than friends—and would hear of no other conclusion—didn't take long for Keiko. He didn't seem bothered by the implication, but then she wondered if he'd spent years insisting on the truth and finally giving up because they wouldn't believe anyway.

"Where's Dad?" Marcus asked once they made their way around the entire room.

"In with Mom," Josh said. "Come on, I'll take you down to her room. She's been pretty impatient to see you and Keiko."

She started to protest that Marcus would obviously want to see his mother alone, but when every head nearby shook in denial, she saw an argument she couldn't win. As they followed his brother down the long hall, Keiko thought about saying something to Marcus about his family's universal belief about the two of them, but she couldn't get herself to do it—especially not with his sibling close enough to overhear them.

In her room, his mother was sitting up in a chair across from her husband, and Marcus' father rose at once. "There you are."

His mother cried out in happiness and refused to hear of not standing to embrace her son. Keiko got tears in her eyes once more as the two hugged as if they'd thought they might not see each other ever again.

She could see where Marcus and his siblings had gotten their good looks. Even obviously ill, his mother had all the markings of beauty from her youth. Thick, mahogany-colored tresses, a classically lovely face with deep brown eyes. His father was tall and handsome with silver hair, his wide shoulders only slightly stooping. "You must be Keiko. We're so pleased to finally meet you, my dear," Stephen Samuels said.

"As am I," Keiko murmured, sniffing.

As it had been with Jordan's family, the endless affection in the form of hugs and kisses was popular in the Samuels clan. Until his mother wrapped her arms around her, drawing her close and looking into her eyes, Keiko could honestly say she'd never felt so overwhelmed by such an outpouring of acceptance. "You're exactly what I expected, sweetheart. I feel like I know you through and through."

"I do, too."

His mother smiled. "You and my son are made for each other. I'd just hoped that was the case before. Now I can see it with my own two eyes. You'll have the most beautiful children…"

"Mom—" Marcus started.

His mother had tenderly cradled her face in her hands, so Keiko couldn't glance at him to see his expression in response to his mother's assumption.

A doctor and nurse entered the room, cutting off Marcus' protest. Keiko knew this was what he'd been waiting for—the full report on his mother's condition. When Dr. Hall realized he was a colleague, he spoke freely of the symptoms that had brought Mrs. Samuels to the emergency room, and the attempted coronary angioplasty that had failed due to a completely blocked artery. Irene had since undergone all the expected tests. Bypass surgery had been determined to be the best course of action. The procedure would be performed Friday morning.

When the nurse asked them to leave the room so she and the doctor could have a look at his mother, Keiko followed Marcus and his father out of the room. "What do you think, son?" Stephen asked, and Keiko could see from his careworn expression that he'd been worried but had probably tried to hide the fact from his wife.

"I think she'll come through fine, Dad. The overall mortality related to CABG is only three to four percent. Mom's strong. She'll get through it and then she'll be better."

His father nodded, clearly reassured. "I wish you could perform the surgery."

Marcus shook his head. "It's not my specialty, Dad. Mom's in good hands. I've looked into Dr. Hall's accreditation. He's the top in his field."

Stephen nodded again, somehow looking older. Keiko recalled that the last time he'd been home, Marcus had been concerned by how his parents had aged. He'd been gone so long, the changes always seemed drastic to him.

"I don't know what I'd do without your mother, Marcus. I'm not sure if I could go on."

Marcus embraced his father with one arm around his shoulders, offering comfort despite appearing slightly worried himself. His mother was in her late sixties and her health was obviously deteriorating. Even still, there was no reason to believe she wouldn't come through the bypass surgery and go on to live for many, many years. Keiko schooled her expression to be as reassuring as Marcus' had been for his father. His gaze met hers, and she saw gratitude as tender as a hug would be between them.

## Chapter 6

"I admit it, I missed this more than I should have." Marc grinned and bit into the double cheeseburger with everything but onions on it. After so many years of foreign food, he almost groaned out loud at the indulgence he could get anywhere, anytime now.

Across from him in the booth, Keiko had ordered a single cheeseburger, no condiments, and the salty crinkle-cut fries Marc had actually craved like an addiction. She smiled at him before *nibbling* into hers. Although she'd ordered a much smaller burger, in her hands the fare looked huge. Like a sucker-punch to the gut, he reacted to the oddly sensual image. They'd been best friends for so long. That he could suddenly be seeing her as anything else made no sense to him. Just watching her eat felt embarrassingly erotic to him. He hoped she'd take his flushed face as nothing more than physical hunger being appeased.

For the next few minutes, they ate together in blissful silence. On the heels of his unexpected arousal, he was starting to feel the effects of 'reliving the same day twice.' Marc took a deep breath, setting down his half-eaten burger. "It's beginning to hit me. I feel like I'm in slow motion."

She nodded, dabbing at her mouth with a napkin. "I can tell you're tired. Why don't you let me drive to Jordan's at least? Are you sure you'll be okay going home?"

He shrugged. "It's only twenty-minutes, a half hour. Don't worry." Despite his reassurance, he wanted to be in his old bed when his jet lag hit—not behind the wheel of a car.

"All things considered, your mother looked very good. The heart attack must have been a surprise for everyone. From all appearances, she's taken good care of herself."

Marc nodded. "She and Dad still walk two miles a day. The only time they don't is in the winter, when the sidewalks aren't plowed and could be icy. They've got this machine that's a cross between a tread mill, a stair-stepper and a ski-glider that they take turns using every day when the weather isn't the best. That said, it probably won't shock you to hear that my family loves good food in enormous quantities—and that includes plenty of just-plain-bad-for-you desserts and fried foods."

Keiko shook her head on a teasing grin. "You'll be in heaven as your family plies you with all you've missed."

"You could say that."

"Should I save you from yourself?"

Marc laughed. "Eventually. Just give me two weeks of everything I've missed for most of twelve years, and I promise I'll start taking care of myself again." In Japan, he'd enjoyed his almost daily workouts. The organization provided a free gym within the dorms. Exercise was a familiar, cheap way to fill the hours of the day when he wasn't on duty. Keiko and Haruki had joined him more often than not, and so it had felt to him like a social event—as if he was getting out and doing something rather than hiding up in his room, where he could better control his panic attacks. Maybe, being home, he would never have a traumatic episode like that again. Maybe the disorder would fade and he'd eventually forget he'd ever suffered in that way. *I can only wish.*

While he finished his meal, he glanced around the

ultra-busy restaurant, noticing the number of attractive women there. Strangely, he found himself comparing them to Keiko—so delicate, graceful, exotic and sweetly sexy. *I wish we didn't have to be apart— even when I crash from the jet lag. I wish she could...crash...with me. Lord, I'm more out of it than I assumed. But I'm forty years old and I've wanted to be with one special woman for so long, I don't know if I can control myself anymore.* His fatigued mind refused to dislodge the image of lying down with petite Keiko enveloped from head to toe inside the cradle of his body, so much larger and stronger than hers. He almost caught his breath in pleasurable agony at the mere thought.

"What is it?" she asked, obviously seeing something in his expression he didn't possess the energy to hide.

"I wish you were staying closer," he admitted.

She didn't speak, but her expression softened so that even without the confirmation of words, he knew *(more pleasurable agony)* that she wanted the same thing. *Is it even in the realm of possibility that she finds me attractive? That, if she felt she had any choice at all which man to be with for the rest of her life, she'd choose* me?

About twenty minutes later, he walked her up to Jordan's doorstep and set down her luggage. "You have my father's phone number?"

Looking slightly ill at ease, she nodded. "And you have Jordan's number?"

"Yeah. I'll have to get a cell phone as soon as I can." *So I can hear your voice whenever I need to— constantly.*

"Let me know when you go to get one. I need one of my own."

As if American air allowed him to return to the old habit, he slipped his hands into his pockets the way he used to—before he'd moved to Japan—when he was nervous. "Well, I'll see you tomorrow—if my jet lag isn't too bad, that is. I'll call you. Or you call me."

Her expression worried, she put her hand on his forearm plaintively. "Please call me when you get home. You have no idea what you look like, Marcus. I want to make sure you get in all right."

He grinned. "What do I look like?"

Keiko abruptly poked him in the chest with her finger. Inflicting damage on him in any physical way wasn't possible. "Like, if I tap you like this, you'll just fall right over backwards."

His head was beginning to spin in that whirly-gig way that was the second level of his extreme jet lag. He laughed out loud, and without thinking—only acting on gut-level instinct—he grasped her wrist and urged her into his arms. He hugged her hard, wrapping both arms fully around her slight form. Without meaning to, he lifted her right off her feet. Dear Lord, she felt good next to him, as if they were adjoining puzzle pieces.

A moment later, when she looked up at him in naked vulnerability, he understood definitely that he wouldn't have the resistance to prevent himself from kissing her if he didn't walk away. *Immediately. And fast as lightning.* "I'll call you as soon as I get home," he promised, setting her down and heading down the sidewalk backward. He waved. She waved back. He got in the car and drove home with her beautiful smile, her wide-open expression, and that sweet little jab to his chest keeping him afloat.

He sighed audibly when he reached Peaceful, a small town that lived up to its name in an old-fashioned, nostalgic sense. *There is no place like home,*

*Dorothy.* His parents lived on the outskirts of town, in the opposite direction as La Crosse, and their family church, which his father had pastored most of his life and his youngest brother now served as shepherd over, was only a few miles from the home Marc had grown up in.

His chest felt tight and heavy with relief once he steered down a familiar street and saw his parents' house at the end. He turned his head as he slowed the car to a crawl in order to take in all that he'd missed. His brother Josh and his family lived next door to their parents. On the opposite side of the street from his brother's was the house of Marc's best friend throughout his school years—Will Peterson. Marc was surprised to see the Peterson home was up for sale. He'd always loved that Craftsman style house. *Where Will and I got into plenty of trouble.*

Chuckling nostalgically, he eased the car up to the realtor box and pulled a flyer out of the holder. Setting it on the passenger's side, he continued on home. He let himself in the front door, set down his luggage and the flyer, and his mind went to Keiko. Not wanting to worry her, he immediately picked up the telephone and called her. She answered on the first ring with his name. "I'm in one piece," he told her.

"Thank God. Now, you better get yourself to bed, Marcus Samuels, before you fall over and spend the next fourteen hours on the hard, cold floor."

Marcus laughed. "I'm going." He would have liked a shower, but he knew Keiko was right. He wouldn't be able to stand much longer.

"Good night, Marcus."

"See you when I come out of the coma."

Their shared joy expanded in his chest as he hung up reluctantly. After rooting through his luggage, he found the melatonin that would help his body clock get back in sync. He climbed the stairs and all but staggered to his bedroom to gratefully find fresh linen on the bed. *Tamara or Justine, taking care of me when Mom isn't able.*

He said a prayer for his mother while he kicked off his shoes and stripped down to his shorts. Lying back beneath the covers, he closed his eyes on a deep sigh. The image of Keiko beside him, wrapped in his arms, filled his mind just before he faded out.

Jordan was a woman with the kind of energy that made everyone around her dizzy. With forest green eyes, short blond hair and a light, flawless complexion, she exuded a brightness that was more than a little ethereal. About five years earlier, she'd almost single-handedly set up a rape counseling clinic, where Marcus' youngest sister Samantha worked as a counselor, but since Jordan and her husband Micah had had their first child, Jordan had become the traditional wife and mother that she'd long ago insisted she never wanted to be. Yet motherhood and marriage obviously suited her. Keiko had never seen her friend so relaxed, lying on her side on the plush carpet contently watching her eleven-month-old cruise around the living room like a whirlwind.

"Is there something you want to tell me, Keiko? I mean, you *resigned* from WMMO! That's major. That's drastic. But you're not even telling me *why* you did it. Unless..."

Keiko tensed slightly from her curled-up place in the corner of the sofa.

"I mean, come on, girlfriend, whenever you came home in the past five years, it was with Marcus Samuels. Was I supposed to overlook that compelling fact?"

"I don't know what you mean," Keiko said, deliberately obtuse. "It was time to resign. My contract—"

Jordan laughed. "You don't need to tell me that again. Your contract was up months ago, I know. But why *now*?"

Little Duffy, named after his grandfather on Jordan's side, army-crawled his way to the area of the floor just below Keiko. With great effort, he pulled himself to standing. Keiko exploded in praise, and the baby laughed as if he'd performed a trick. He was so adorable, strong and sturdy, a perfect amalgamation of his mommy and daddy.

Jordan was shaking her head, for once out of the moment with her son's progress. "I don't see why you have to marry that pervert, Keiko. I mean, you've put off a lot of Japanese traditions, haven't you, in becoming a Christian? Why should you care about some promise you made before you were truly capable of making up your own mind? Surely your parents can't hold you to something like that, especially considering what he does for a living?"

Jordan had never possessed the slightest degree of patience where Japanese customs, traditions or duties were concerned. Not the way Marcus had right from the beginning and even up to the end of his time in her native country. Keiko kept her gaze fixed on the baby.

"Do you think Marc is attractive?"

*I didn't expect that.* "What do you mean?"

"Look, I've never met him personally..." Jordan sat up, crossing her legs. "But I've met most of the other

Samuels' brothers. They're gorgeous. Drop *dead* gorgeous. Why should Marc be any different?"

"He's not," Keiko admitted, smiling goofily down at Duff cutting his teeth on her jeans and generally drooling like mad.

"So...! What's the problem?" Jordan demanded.

"No problem."

"You know what I mean, Keiko Oichi. What obstacle is keeping the two of you apart? He *must* find you attractive."

Keiko giggled. "Why must he?"

Her friend blinked at her like her question had been pure stupidity. "Um, because you are!"

Keiko shook her head, grinning just a little as she lifted Duff onto her lap. "He's never said anything about how I look." *Mostly. He's been polite. And sweet. I'm sure he didn't mean anything all the times he complimented me.*

"But he does find you attractive," Jordan said stubbornly.

Even as Duffy got interested in the pearly buttons on her blouse, Keiko felt slightly breathless at the idea that Marcus might find her attractive. Sometimes when he was tired or his guard was down, as it'd been at the restaurant and then when he'd dropped her off here, he looked at her so strangely. So deliciously. She couldn't prevent herself from believing that his feelings became transparent during those times. He'd held her like he'd been waiting insanely for the first opportunity to get her in his arms. *He wanted to kiss me. That was why he walked away so fast. How can I consider anything else? He's never looked at me like that before, looked at my mouth with the kind of heat in his eyes... The kind I don't know anything about—but want to. With him.* Keiko swallowed guiltily at her thoughts, not willing to look at her friend for fear of exposing every last ounce of her recent confusion.

Jordan sighed. "Unfortunately, we'll have to continue this conversation another time."

"Not on my account."

Jordan mock-glared at her. "Duff's got a play group. And you need to get some sleep."

"I'm fine."

"Sure you are. But a nap would do you good."

When Jordan scooped her son away from her to change his diaper and get him ready for their outing, Keiko uncontrollably felt bereft. She didn't often get to hold babies, but whenever she did she knew she wanted one of her own. Unlikely prospect as that seemed, her longing for a child grew constantly.

"We'll be back in a couple hours. You'll have the house to yourself. Enjoy yourself." Jordan shrugged, ever the matchmaking instigator. "Call Marc. Whatever."

Jordan would be trying to fix her up with Marcus Samuels the entire time she stayed here. While that pressure wouldn't be comfortable, Keiko disliked the idea of going 'home' to her apartment in Chicago even more. Knowing his jet lag would force him to sleep for the next fourteen hours or more, she would miss Marcus enough as it was. At the moment, she couldn't be certain when she'd be ready to go to her designated home in the States, but she knew eventually she'd have to. *If Marcus finds someone to date, someone he wants to be his girlfriend and eventually his wife and the mother of his children...* Keiko would think no further than that she wanted to be close to him, especially while his mother was ill. Unfortunately, even Jordan's home seemed too far from him to appease her constant craving to be in his presence.

She took her luggage into the guest bedroom and unpacked, then took a long, hot shower. That luxury assured her that getting spoiled again by the ease of the West would be only too easy. She was able to sleep a few hours, just as Jordan had predicted, but she woke feeling the emotion that always prevailed whenever she came home with Marcus for a vacation and the two of them went their separate ways. She felt adrift, bereft, lost without him in her life each and every day. *What would I do if it had to be that way permanently or nearly so?*

Keiko caught her breath. What would she do if Marcus found a woman he wanted to spend his life with? The thought was complete and utter torment. How could she go on? Pretend that... *What? That I don't wish that woman was* me*? How? It's not possible for us to be that way together...and yet, if Marcus showed the slightest interest...* Keiko swallowed, aware that he'd done that and more since she'd admitted she'd resigned to be with him. *I could never, ever refuse him anything. Because, although I haven't been willing to let myself even consider the possibility, he's the only man I can imagine myself being with. I don't want to hurt him. Despite wishing fervently otherwise, I am engaged. And I certainly don't want to set myself up for a fall if I end up unable to refuse my parents or Ryu.*

But what if Marcus admitted that he found her attractive and wanted to be with her romantically, in a passionate love she could hardly conceive of but contradictorily had to admit she desired with him alone? Keiko closed her eyes against the hopeful yearning that filled her entire being like blinding light introduced in a deep, dark place. *If only...* But she didn't dare, did she?

## Chapter 7

The next evening Keiko became poignantly aware of her own internal restlessness bouncing around her chest until a part of her wanted to scream to get it to stop. She'd had a full night's rest the night before, surprising herself since she rarely slept so many hours, even following travel. She'd spent the day with Jordan and Duffy, falling in love with the little bundle of sweetness—so that each time she looked at him, she was filled with a kind of agony that was uncomfortable because she had no prospects for fulfilling the burgeoning need inside her. She'd spent her lifetime pursuing her career and a robust education that fell in perfect alignment with all her parents had wanted for her. But she'd realized she was ready to be done with the whole thing. As Jordan had, Keiko was ready for a husband and family and all things domestic.

"Did you call Haruki?" Jordan asked while they were preparing dinner. Samantha, her husband Kyle and their little girl about the same age as Duff would be joining them for the evening meal. Then Keiko planned to accompany Samantha to the hospital to visit Mrs. Samuels.

"I suppose I'd better," Keiko murmured. She'd been putting that task off, uncertain what her brother would say. He'd acted so strangely at the airport when he'd sent her and Marcus off. She wondered often if he believed she was betraying everything Japanese. She worried that he might revert to the old ways they'd practiced mildly while growing up. She'd known more than a few Japanese Christians who'd eventually merged their Christianity with Shinto or Hinduism, as if Christ could co-exist willingly with false gods. What if her decision to accompany Marcus to America for an indefinite stay pushed her brother in that backward direction? Would that mean she'd sinned?

When she went to the back of the house for some privacy and dialed her brother's cell phone, she only got his voice mail. She quickly left a message, letting him know she and Marcus had gotten in all right and everything was fine. She asked him to call her, then hung up. The doorbell pealed, and she shook herself out of the annoying restlessness she couldn't explain.

By the time Keiko arrived at the front of the house once more, Jordan had answered the door. Duff and baby Irene were hugging each other while being held in their mothers' arms. As soon as they separated, Samantha turned to Keiko and hugged her. Somehow Irene ended up in her arms, and Keiko couldn't help being charmed by the tiny beauty who had all the Samuels' best traits.

"Have you talked to Marcus?" Keiko asked his sister.

Samantha shook her head. "He won't come up for air for a few hours yet. I called Daddy just before we left home, and he said Marc was still sleeping. How about you? Are you still jet-lagged?"

"I recovered remarkably well."

"I can see that. You look gorgeous. Not that you didn't yesterday at the hospital."

Keiko laughed. "I don't know about that."

After saying they would get dinner on the table, the two women encouraged Keiko to watch the two babies, and she did so gratefully. Each time she laughed at their antics, she also felt tears pressing ruthlessly against the backs of her eyes. *Marcus will have babies this beautiful. Marcus and his wife...*

She missed him throughout the delicious, delightful meal and more so whenever anyone mentioned anything about him. Although she was well aware that his mother had long ago jumped to the wrong conclusion about her and Marcus, she'd never felt compelled to disillusion her. She'd told herself she couldn't be sure Irene believed they were a couple, so what was the point of bringing up a non-subject? But an hour and a half later in her hospital room, Irene asked Keiko to sit with her—alone.

For a long minute, Irene Samuels simply stared at her with love and joy in her expression. "It's so obvious to me that you and Marcus are in love, Keiko. You can't imagine how happy that makes me. I know my son gave his life to the Lord and he was willing to wait to fulfill his own needs. But he's longed for love and a family. Now he's finally found the woman of his dreams."

Keiko could hardly breathe as everything inside her insisted she be honest with Marcus' mother. She couldn't force the words out of her mouth. Nothing seemed able to pass through the blockage that filled her throat.

"You may not know the truth of his feelings for you yet, but I know my son, sweetheart."

Keiko stared, tears welling hotly behind her eyes.

"I know when my son is in love. And he is now. Each time he talked about you all these years, whenever he looked at you when you came to visit yesterday, the truth of his feelings became clearer to me. I can assure you that he'll make you a wonderful husband and father, just as he's made a wonderful friend to you all these years."

His mother's insight was her undoing. Unable to help herself, she blatantly showed the dear woman with her misting eyes that something as-yet-undefined between her and Marcus had changed. *Can I be what he needs? Can I even let myself consider it?*

"What does your heart tell you, Keiko?" his mother asked softly, holding her hand tenderly between her own dry, papery ones.

She swallowed. "I...I don't know."

His mother nodded in understanding—something Keiko didn't feel capable of grasping herself. "Then listen to whatever your heart tells you, sweetheart. You'll know the answer if you just listen."

*That's the whole problem. I've been listening. For the first time, I've actually listened to my own heart. I've been afraid to accept what I've been hearing it say to me.*

When Samantha and Kyle dropped her off at Jordan's later, Keiko knew unequivocally that she was in danger—in danger of falling in love with every single member of Marcus' family for certain. But most of all, she was in danger of letting herself fall in love with Marcus himself. She hadn't allowed that possibility to rise anywhere to the surface up to this point. *I must have realized deep down that it would be too easy. If I let myself go an inch, I would cross the barrier I tried to keep between us if only in my heart or mind. I knew I'd cross over to the point of no return before I blinked, and then it would be too late to turn back.*

Inside Jordan and Micah's house, soft lamps glowed in the living room. She knew they were already in bed, knew she was alone. Even as she acknowledged that hearing Marcus' voice would only make her more confused and needy, she felt desperate for him.

After walking to the phone, she picked the receiver up and dialed his father's house. She recognized Stephen's low voice, recognized the sorrow and uncertainty in his tone.

"I hope it's not too late to call, Mr. Samuels. It's Keiko."

"It's fine, dear, but unfortunately my son is still comatose."

Keiko giggled softly. "Then don't bother him. I just wanted to...call. Tomorrow is soon enough. How are you?"

"Holding up."

"It's okay if you're not," she told him. "You can be strong for your wife, but when you're alone with the Lord..."

"You're right. I haven't been allowing myself that. I've been afraid..."

"...you'll fall apart altogether?" she guessed, her tone tender as she reached out to him the only way she could.

"Yes. You understand."

*Before a few days ago, I would have said that I've* never *been in danger of losing anyone I love and so I couldn't understand his feelings. But when I accepted a hundred percent that Marcus was leaving Japan and I might never see him again, everything inside me changed. I out-and-out panicked.* "Yes, I understand. My heart and prayers are with you and your family."

"Thank you, Keiko. My children have always made wise decisions in choosing mates. Marcus found a treasure in you, my dear."

The lump in her throat grew. She pressed her fingers to her mouth to hold back the rising sob. *Why do I feel this way? Does it make any sense to be so out-of-control?*

"As soon as he's awake, I'll tell Marcus you called. Good night, Keiko."

"Good night," she whispered shakily.

Marc woke to darkness and disorientation. For long minutes as the grogginess passed, he wondered where he was. Japan? Had it all been a dream that he and Keiko had come home, together, for good? *For life? Maybe even for love?*

He reached for the touch lamp beside him, fully prepared to see the unbearably small dorm room he'd occupied for so long. Instead, he saw the pea green bed his oldest brother Peter had slept in on the opposite side of the room they'd shared as teenagers. Nostalgia crept over him, and he found himself chuckling at the memory of his decision to paint Pete's bed to match the rest of the god-awful furniture in the cramped room. His deed had been a statement of rebellion at always getting hand-me-downs instead of new things—a pastor's salary didn't stretch nicely to cover six kids. His parents hadn't capitulated and purchased the new items the way he'd hoped. And Pete hadn't been all that thrilled with him for turning his bed into a duplicate of the rest of the junk in their shared room. Lucky for him, Peter had never been able to stay mad at him—even after all the crazy stunts Marc had dragged his unwitting brother along for.

*I'm home. And come hell or high water, I'm not going back.* He winced slightly. *Okay, maybe not* hell...

He glanced at the clock. Seven-thirty. But what day was it? As he swung his legs out from under the covers, he picked up the alarm clock cube on the nightstand and squinted at the date. *Tuesday.* He'd slept through last night and then practically this whole day.

Thoughts of his mother and Keiko crowded in. Rising, he didn't bother to put on more than the boxers he'd slept in. He went down the stairs, following the light shining in the living room. He found his father in his old arm chair, a Greek Bible open in his lap. His expression had wandered off from the book, out the open curtains, blindly into the growing darkness.

When Marc stepped on a loose, creaky floorboard, his father's head swung around to him. "Oh, you're awake. Feel better?"

Marc raised an eyebrow. "Could do with another eight hours," he offered, only slightly kidding. "How's Mom?"

"Still holding her own. Tamara's spending the night at the hospital with her."

"You didn't have to stay home on my account. You could have stayed with Mom."

His father shook his head. "We've been switching off. It's Tamara's night."

Conceding, Marc nodded.

"Keiko called."

Pleasure flooded him. "She did?"

"She just wanted to know how you were doing. She went over to see your mother earlier this evening."

More warmth spread through him. What would he do without her?

"She didn't want to bother you. She said she'd call again tomorrow."

Marc nodded. In the past, Keiko had told him she didn't suffer from the jet lag as dramatically as he did. Would she be awake?

"Are you hungry, son?"

"Actually I'm starving. But I really need a shower

first."

"I'll make omelets."

The one meal his father made well that wasn't straight from the charcoal grill was a bacon and cheddar cheese omelet. When Marc had been a very small kid and his mother had gone away to visit relatives or for some other reason, the family had practically lived on omelets until they were old enough to learn how to cook themselves.

The wayward thought, *What would Dad do without Mom? Eat omelets for every meal?* made Marc feel hollow. He didn't want to think like that. His mother would pull through the surgery. She had to.

"I missed dinner myself," his father continued. "You get cleaned up. The food will be ready when you come out."

"Thanks, Dad."

Marc took a long, hot shower, pushing away unproductive thoughts. Instead, his mind went to Keiko and areas he knew he shouldn't let himself go into. What would she do if he told her the truth? That he wanted their relationship to be more than friendship? His memories of previous relationships— the ones he'd had as a teenager and while in college and medical school—haunted him too much not to make him wary. He'd always jumped in too fast, eyes closed, hoping he and the woman reached the same conclusion about the outcome of their romance. *Monogamy and the whole nine yards with marriage and kids.* He couldn't remember whether he'd had few options or he'd made choices that weren't wise when it came to the women he dated. They'd all wanted to spend the first part of their adult years pursuing a career. Once they were successful, the very tentative plan had been to start a family.

Marc had begun to think there were no females like his mother and older sister anymore—the kind who wanted to be a mother and wife, devoting herself to those roles. To even *think* about wanting that in the woman he spent his life with was no longer politically correct for a man. It'd become wrong-thinking for a guy to take care of his family by supporting them financially, to give his wife the option of not having to be in the workforce so she could devote herself to their children.

Marc wasn't sure why so many women refused to consider that, but he supposed the bottom line came down to an issue of trust. With good reason, women didn't like to be put in the position of not having the means to support themselves financially—because these days, things went wrong more often in marriage than right. And then there was the fact that many women were made to feel like they'd failed if they couldn't or didn't want to try juggling a full-time job, children, husband, and a household.

Wryly, Marc recalled that his relationships had all been brief once he'd admitted what he hoped for in the future. He found he could barely remember the names of any of the girls he'd dated. *A man who eagerly desires a lifelong commitment yet has never had a serious relationship in his life—that's gotta be one for the books. But I have had a serious relationship...with Keiko. I can't let her count, even if I want to more than anything.*

After his shower, he dressed in comfortable sleep pants. In the hall, he could hear his father puttering around in the kitchen below. Omelets had always been a production that he'd loved to watch when he was younger. His need to hear Keiko's voice was stronger now. He tiptoed to the end of the hall, into his father's study. Along the way, he hit just about every creaky floorboard. He expected his father to call up to him, but he didn't.

Marc picked up the phone and dialed Jordan and Micah's phone number. He had no idea what to say. Keiko answered the phone on the first ring. She must have seen the number on Caller ID because she greeted him by name. "Marcus," she breathed warmly—might as well have been right into his tingling ear. "How do you feel?"

"Better. But still groggy." He knew he sounded stiff but couldn't help it. The sound of her voice had erupted fissures of excitement over every inch of his flesh.

"One more night's sleep, and you'll be fine, I'm sure."

"How about you? What were you doing?" Marc realized he was talking in a low, husky voice, as if he was afraid someone would overhear him. *And if anyone did, they'd know I'm in the danger zone here. When did a phone conversation become the height of erotica? Why does just her voice put me in this state every single time lately? Seeing her... I'm completely out of control.*

"Truthfully? Duffy woke up just after I got in from seeing your mother. Instead of letting him disturb Jordan and Micah, who must have had an exhausting day to be in bed so early, I went in to him. He just needed a little cuddling."

The image of Keiko with a baby in her arms was almost painful in its poignancy. "Are you still holding him?" he asked, choked up and not even sure why.

"He's asleep in my arms right now. He's such an angel. So is your mother's namesake. I've fallen hard for both of them."

"Little Irene is a doll. I met Samantha and Kyle's baby for the first time at the hospital yesterday. The pictures coming through e-mail...well, you know. It's just not the same. I've missed so much."

"There's time to make up for it. Just have faith."

She'd read his mind. Again. They were so connected, sometimes it blew his mind.

"I saw your mother. She's glad you're getting the sleep you need."

"I need to see her."

"Do you want to meet for a late breakfast tomorrow morning? Then we can go see her together."

"I can't wait." He knew he put too much intense emotion into those words and quickly added, "Have you called Haruki to let him know we got in all right?"

"I left a message. He didn't answer and hasn't called me back."

Marc grimaced. "He's really furious with me, isn't he?"

"With *you*? It's *me* he's furious with. Because the idea of marrying Ryu is..."

Marc heard her swallow with great difficulty, and his teeth clenched on his own emotions concerning her insane betrothal.

"...*death*...to me. Haruki thinks I'm betraying both Japanese and family tradition by not wanting to marry Ryu."

"Are you considering breaking the engagement?" Marc couldn't hold himself back from asking. He knew the hope in his voice was too...well, *hopeful*.

"You don't know, Marcus. I can't bear the thought that he'll ever call for me. But I can't imagine facing my parents either, to tell them there's no way I can live up to my duty. That I would rather die."

"Isn't it fundamentally wrong to make plans that

you expect your children have to carry out as adults? Children aren't capable of making larger-than-life choices, and shouldn't they be allowed to make *their own* decisions, follow *their own* path, only if and when they're ready?"

"That's American thinking."

"To me, it's *right* thinking," he muttered, his frustration bleeding through. He'd had a twelve-year bellyful of tolerating irrational, even ridiculous customs that should have been abandoned long ago.

Surprising him, Keiko laughed quietly in his sensitive-where-she-was-concerned ear. "You're coming out of your refined shell, Marcus Samuels. I don't think you've been honest with yourself or anyone else these past dozen years about all the rules and regulations involved in living in Japan."

He sighed, rubbing his eyes. "I couldn't be rude— but you have to admit it's far too easy to be rude without having the slightest intention of being that way over there. Besides, the last thing in the world I wanted was to offend you. I don't want to do that now. You mean too much to me, Keiko."

"You couldn't offend me. That's not even possible. Don't you know that by now? Besides, I'm liking this slightly less refined man. I can't wait to see what else emerges from that shell of yours, Marcus Samuels."

Arousal electrified him at her words. Could he say or do anything he wanted with this woman? Could he open his heart and tell her how close he was to falling truly, madly, deeply, *irrevocably* in love with her? If she gave him the slightest leeway, he'd be putty in this incredible woman's hands.

## Chapter 8

By the time Marcus pulled up to the curb outside Jordan and Micah's house, Keiko could hardly breathe. She wanted to see him so badly, her heart all but jumped right out of her chest. The only thing in the world she needed was to look upon his perfect face, to be enveloped in his accepting, loving arms.

He parked and was out of the car in seconds, looking full of life and energy. If she'd had any air in her lungs, the meager amount would have been sucked straight up into her brain. *Dear Lord, he's gorgeous.* In Japan, he'd worn professional clothing that he kept in excellent condition the twelve years he lived there. He hadn't wanted to spend money trying to track down his size in a country that didn't outfit men as tall and muscular as he was. But here at home, he was able to wear old, faded blue jeans that might have been left over from his life before he became a medical missionary. The jeans fit him like a dream, showcasing his muscular, long legs. With the plaid button-down shirt he wore over a plain white t-shirt, he seemed relaxed and happy, in his element the way he'd never quite managed in Japan.

"You're beautiful, Keiko," he surprised her by saying when they met on the sidewalk.

She'd put on fashionable white denim trousers with a spray of rhinestones along the seams, a spring-light, heather gray V-neck sweater and open-toed pumps. Even as she blushed she was giggling, he was apologizing, and she shook her head. "Don't be sorry. Thank you. We get to dress like this so infrequently, don't we? It feels good. You look good." She laughed again, punctuating the dizzy feeling in her head. "I'm starving!"

"Good. So am I."

He took her to a Belgian waffle house, and she'd barely finished half of one fruit-topped concoction to his three before she groaned, "I'm going to be so fat in a month."

Grinning, he shook his head. "You've lived in the United States for years, and you've never gotten close to fat. Have you?"

"I've been diligent. That's the only reason," she insisted.

They laughed together, and Marcus abruptly looked past her, an expression of pleased surprise on his face. She turned to look over her shoulder and found a man coming toward them with a welcoming smile on his boyishly freckled face. Marcus stood for some hearty, male backslapping. "Will Peterson. It's been a lifetime." He introduced the two of them, telling her, "Keiko, Will and I were best friends growing up in Peaceful."

She scooted over, waving to Marcus' side of the booth opposite her. "Please join us, Will."

Marcus slid in next to her and filled their shared space with his wonderfully wide shoulders. Before long, he and Will were getting caught up. Marcus had leaned back and casually put his arm across the back of the booth—not touching her but making her almost insanely aware of the possessive shelter he'd constructed over her. Keeping herself from leaning back against him, breathing deeply of his potent cologne, required every ounce of her shaky willpower.

She expected that one of them would eventually get around to the topic of girlfriend, wife, kids, but surprisingly, neither did. The conversation instead meandered into realty, and Keiko remembered Marcus telling her he wanted to buy a house—and even thought he could afford one.

"I was surprised to see the old house up for sale. When did your parents move?"

Will looked pained. "Dad died a few months ago."

"I'm sorry to hear that," Marcus murmured with feeling.

"Yeah. Thanks. Mom moved in with her sister—"

"Aunt Trudy of the hundred cats?"

Will chuckled. "And the mysteriously disappearing gerbils. I'm living and working in La Crosse and haven't been back to the old house much. I know Ma wants me to live there, but... It's not feasible. Even still, I don't want it to fall into disrepair, so I'm eager to sell it."

"Is your Mom all right with that?"

Keiko could sense Marcus' growing interest as he sat forward, leaning both arms on the scarred tabletop.

"She is. If neither of us can live in it, she sees no point in holding on to it. Some nice, young family is preferable to letting the property become overgrown and unused. For that reason, I'm very motivated to sell."

"You know...I'm motivated to *buy*."

His old friend seemed surprised. "Buy the old house? But I thought you were off doing medical evangelism in China?"

"Japan."

"Japan. That's what I said. When would you have time to live in the house?"

"I'm back home for good. And I'll need a place to live. I love that old house, Will. We had many adventures there, my friend."

Will grinned. "Adventures? I think our mothers would have called them something a little more troublesome."

Marcus laughed heartily, glancing at Keiko. "When we were nine, we decided to take Will's dad's three-wheeler out for a spin."

"That was back in the days when three-wheelers actually only had three wheels and weren't loftily called ATVs," Will injected.

"Anyway, we were tearing around the backyard something good..."

"My backyard and part of Marc's mom's garden. I think I can still hear Ma screaming at us from the back porch over the mass, wanton destruction of..."

Both men hooted and chimed in unison, "...innocent vegetables."

Covering her mouth with her hand, Keiko giggled, picturing her strait-laced, ultra-polite Marcus doing anything of the kind. The three of them laughed off and on over the next minute as the men proclaimed the memory "good times."

"Anyway, the house is for sale, Marc, and I'd rather sell it to a friend than a stranger. Ma would like that, too. If you want it, it's yours, buddy."

Marcus glanced at her, seeming impressed with the offer. "I was never any good at haggling. Are you sure, Will? You'd be willing to take the asking price?"

"At this point, I really want to unload it. Lot of great memories there and selling it in the first place wasn't an easy decision for me. But the way I look at it now, if you buy it, I'll still get to see it sometimes."

"Anytime."

Will reached into his back pocket and pulled out his wallet. "Why don't you give my realtor a call. We'll get something set up." He handed over a business card.

Marcus nodded. "I'll do it today. Good to see you, Will."

When the other man got up, he and Keiko exchanged friendly goodbyes. Will walked away, and Keiko noticed again how close she and Marcus were sitting. She secretly hoped he wouldn't think to move to the other side of the booth once more. "Are you really considering the purchase of a house?" Keiko asked him when he turned her way.

"I saw the realty sheets last night, and it's definitely in my price range—especially if Will is serious about accepting his asking price. I can't live with my parents forever, right? This house is everything I want. Family next door along with privacy when I need it."

Keiko blushed at his words, looking away to neatly fold her napkin and straw wrapping. *Someday Marcus will need privacy...with a girlfriend or wife.*

They visited his mother, who beamed like the sunshine at the sight of them together. "My hold-out son is finally in love," she said when she hugged him. Surprisingly, he didn't bother arguing with her. Instead, he asked her if she understood the surgery she'd be having on Friday morning, how she felt about it. She displayed the kind of faith and acceptance of everything going according to the Lord's will that Marcus himself wasn't always capable of having. His optimism had been lacking of late.

"I'm not sure I'm ready to drop you off," Marcus said a few hours later, once they returned to his parents' old car.

Keiko smiled across the seat at him. "I'd love to see your parents' house and your friend Will's house—at least from the outside."

Her suggestion was met with a pleased smile. He

drove there and then gave her the grand tour of his parents' home, including his old bedroom. "This is exactly how it looked when you were a teenager, isn't it?"

"How did you know?"

"Maybe you're still a fan of...The Crusaders?"

He looked truly chagrined and laughed. Together they walked downstairs and Keiko ran her hand over the smooth wood of the upright piano. "Let me guess: Your family sang Christmas carols together around this beauty every year?"

"We still do. And we all took piano lessons. My mom taught them. You know, if you and Haruki hadn't taken me to those performances in Japan over the years..."

"You would never have gotten any culture at all?" she teased.

He grinned at her, clearly conceding to her assessment of his tendency toward reclusiveness.

As if by mutual decision, they both sat on the bench, and he played an easy classical piece with more than a few clunkers. "I guess it's not like riding a bicycle."

She glanced up at him to see he was already looking at her, his expression fun, completely unserious. Off the top of her head, Keiko demanded, "Why didn't you set your mother straight?"

"About what?"

She swallowed, feeling suffocated and strangled with the craziness in her head. *Change the subject. Don't try to go where you're forbidden to go.* "About us."

He turned once more to the keys. After an excruciating minute in which she wanted to fly from the house and hide in any available hole, he asked softly, "Why did you come home with me, Keiko? Are you staying in the States? For good? And don't say you don't know again."

"I want to stay. Will you ever go back to Japan?"

"If I did, there's only one reason I would ever go back."

"Haruki?" she guessed, but she knew the answer long before he gave it. Her heart spoke and she heard the words loud and clear.

"I would go back with you, Keiko."

"To missionary work?"

He shook his head.

A little raggedly, she teased, "You would hate every minute of any trip back there."

His intense gaze held hers, his expression naked and vulnerable. "We'd be together in the missionary work. Maybe I could cope like I did before. You saved me from myself in that regard before, you know. And I realized when you said you wanted to come home with me that that's all I want. For us to be together. Is that why you came with me, Keiko? Because you realized the same thing? Because you want us to be together, too?"

*"Listen to your heart. You'll know the answer if you just listen."* Keiko took a long, deep, shaky breath and then spoke out loud the word that formed in her head, "Yes."

Marcus closed his eyes in obvious relief. His head moved an inch closer, but his eyes never wavered from hers. "Then tell me you're having doubts about that insane betrothal."

"Since I became a Christian, all I've had are doubts about it."

"Since you became a Christian?"

"Since I became a Christian...and since I met you."

This time, he was the one who swallowed as if

emotions had crammed into his throat and were making it hard for him to talk or even breathe. "Keiko...can I kiss you?"

"Don't ask me," she begged. "Just..." *Let's not analyze this. Let's not think it through. Let's just...enjoy what we have together, whatever it is, wherever it leads.*

He clearly saw her words as telling him he didn't need an invitation. He moved. His lips touched hers. For a long moment, they simply held together, breath and wishes comingled. Then she put her arms around his neck, he put his around her waist, and they fused like molten lead. In an instant, all became one—one heart, one mind, one thought, one wish, one desire.

She'd told herself she would never consider, *had* never considered, Marcus in this way, and yet she realized she'd always known his mouth would be this firm, this demanding, this seductive. She'd always known that to be in his arms was to be home, to be exactly where she wanted to be forever, sheltered and cherished and loved. She'd always known that if they ever kissed, she would fall instantly in love with him— as if she'd been in that state all her life and had just waited for the moment to make the emotion solidified and vibrantly alive, sending her soaring on the wings of such perfection.

*I never want this to end.* When she opened her eyes, she read the same fervent thought in his gaze. Whatever they were doing, whatever road they were on, it was too late to stop and turn back. Their newborn love was too impossibly strong for either of them to deny.

"You're too far away," Marc said the instant Keiko slipped into the passenger seat of the car the next morning and they were in each other's arms. She'd been waiting on the curb when he pulled up.

He hadn't allowed himself to consider that things would change overnight between them. Most certainly, he hadn't wanted to consider that she might have regrets, inhibitions, even unwillingness to continue what they'd started last night. The way she'd kissed him had convinced him she didn't have any of those things. He wouldn't allow any of his own to surface because he already knew he was lost in the possibilities of what he and Keiko could be to one another.

His lips found hers. Together they danced, delved, became desperate for all and everything. She kissed him back with the same eagerness that had fueled his dreams all night. Had her dreams strayed into his and they'd shared them over the distance? He couldn't believe anything else but that. This was too perfect. His entire life felt altered each time their lips fused. He knew without a doubt that his subconscious mind had been working on this very fantasy all the years he'd known this woman. He'd held back...until this time. Now he understood that he loved her. Wildly. He couldn't think straight for that love, for his desire to be with her. He'd been in love with her for years, waiting for it to be right for them. What else mattered now? His only fear was that something else might matter.

He also had no trouble realizing that this was exactly what Haruki had been afraid of—perhaps he'd even seen something between him and Keiko that they hadn't admitted even to themselves. Still, Marc couldn't understand why the man who'd been his close friend for more than a decade would be so threatened at the prospect of him getting involved with his sister. Haruki had to believe that Marc would take much better care of her and treat her the way she deserved—the way her betrothed couldn't and wouldn't. Once more, Marc could only conclude that Japanese customs, duties and obligations were taking hold of even a Christian as strong as Haruki was in his faith.

"You're too far away," he said again when he eased back, panting, and rested his forehead against hers.

"How could we be any closer?" she murmured, obviously believing he meant their immediate proximity. His hand cradled her neck, and she moaned softly when he caressed the satiny skin. His entire body reacted to the purring sound.

"No. Here. With Jordan. I wish you could be closer to me."

"I do, too. Should I get an apartment...?"

The words "Marry me" leapt to the tip of his tongue and he only just held them back for fear of scaring her. His heart was moving at the speed of light. He should have been breathless at his own reckless careening here, but he wasn't. He'd never felt more invigorated in his entire life, so ready and raring to take off for places unknown, hitherto unexplored... He couldn't imagine that she would be comfortable with going from the first kiss to nuptials literally overnight. But he knew he wouldn't be able to wait much longer to bring up that very subject.

"I realize you just met my family, Keiko, but I know my brother Josh and his wife Justine wouldn't mind if you stayed with them for a little while."

"They live right next door to your parents?"

Marc nodded, tracing his finger down the delicate curve of her face to her pointed little chin. She was so beautiful, it was difficult to imagine how... *Okay, how I kept my hands off her all these years. I wish I could stroke every inch of her. Kiss her everywhere.*

"You think they wouldn't mind?"

"I don't think they would at all. In fact, you might be doing them a favor. Josh was talking yesterday about how he got this huge order for rocking chairs last week and Justine has a case going to trial this week... I know they would probably both love it if they had a built-in babysitter for Isaiah, especially for the next couple weeks while they're involved in their individual projects."

"I would love that. Last night felt...far away for me, too."

"Tell me you're not thinking about going to your apartment in Chicago anytime soon."

"You could go with me," she suggested hopefully.

"To help you move?"

Her smile was so brilliant and strangely soft that he couldn't refrain from kissing her again until they were both gasping for air.

"Yes... I think I'm ready to move," she said with her head on his shoulder.

Marc closed his eyes tightly, shuddering slightly, when her fingers uncertainly danced across his chest. He clutched that hand to his heart, knowing he was already on the edge at her sweetly sensual caress.

"There's nothing for me in Chicago. We could go back together, Marcus. Get my things. Go to WMMO headquarters and say goodbye to everyone. Dan was talking about a farewell party for you, wasn't he?"

Marc shook his head definitively. "For *us*, but... No. I'm not ready for that. I don't trust Dan's hold over me at this point. I'm not going back, and there's nothing he can do to change that. But I don't trust him not to try—

by devious methods, if need be."

"You're one of the best doctor's he's ever sent out into the field. You're also a natural evangelist. You can't expect him to be happy about letting you go."

"You're all of those things, too. He didn't give you half as much grief."

Keiko chuckled. "I'm a good doctor, but I use my skills from my hands and my head. My heart isn't in it, the way it is with you. You made every one of those children a part of your life, and they knew it. It's easy for me to hold a piece of myself apart. Do my job. Not get involved. I've done that everywhere, with nearly everyone, for most of my life. It's my way. But you couldn't do that to save your life. It's what made you such an invaluable medical missionary. You heal the whole person. I can only heal the body."

Marc couldn't deny that he'd noticed she was a very competent doctor—and that her style of ministering was radically different from his. Even the way she'd witnessed for Christ had been academic. He'd always appreciated that because the Japanese culture responded to professionalism, even cold-bloodedness, so much better than to his emotional, passionate viewpoints. "Will you continue in medicine after this, honey?"

She turned her head so her chin rested on his chest. "Will you?"

Marc leaned back on the seat slightly. "I was actually thinking that Peaceful doesn't have a pediatric medical environment. We have only a general clinic. I think setting up an office for Peaceful residents to bring their kids would be ideal. Maybe we could do that together."

Her eyes sparkled. "Really? Oh, Marcus, that sounds perfect. I would... It's everything I could have imagined."

He smiled. "Great. But later. After things settle down and we've had more time to relax and enjoy life back home."

She nodded. "Are you still afraid that God doesn't intend for you to have this life you're imagining for yourself now? Your own peds clinic right in your hometown? Your family surrounding you on a daily basis? The promise of a personal life? Do you think He'll take all that away and send you back to Japan or somewhere else you don't want to be?"

He sighed. "I know—Christianity and superstitions don't mingle. I can't seem to help feeling this way. Like everyone else in the world is entitled to life, liberty, and the pursuit of happiness, and I can only move in the small box God's got me locked up in." The fact that his grim, black thoughts had made it outside of his own head should have filled him with utter shame. But for the first time he felt like he could talk to someone about his emotions, however illogical and ludicrous they were. "I realize I'm so blessed that it's a crime for me not to be through-and-through grateful. And I am appreciative. But I guess it's my personality to be pessimistic about ever making my own dreams come true."

"Even as you encourage everyone around you optimistically."

Marc laughed at her extremely optimistic view of him.

"Maybe you'll get everything you ever wanted," Keiko insisted stubbornly. "Maybe the Lord is guiding you toward that now."

"From your lips to God's ear." Did she have any idea that the thing he wanted most was *her*? His need to be with her consumed him now until all he could think about was having her in his life permanently. Making her his willing and happy wife, the mother of his children.

"So, what are we doing today?" she asked. "I'm up for anything."

"I was hoping you'd say that. After breakfast, I have an appointment with my buddy Will and his realtor. We're meeting them at the house. I thought we'd go see my mother just before lunch. And we need cell phones. If there's time, I want to get a car. My own."

She nodded. "I was thinking the same thing. That I need a car."

"I'm happy to be your chauffeur, my lady."

She smiled. "But it would be more convenient for everyone if we both had our own vehicles."

He nodded. "Probably."

Though he didn't need it, they took a tour of Will's parents' home. Other than the fact that there was no furniture, appliances or decoration, it looked exactly as it had when Marc had hung out there as a kid. He loved everything as he had then. Will had obviously taken care not to let the place fall into complete disrepair during the time it'd been empty. Other than needing a new coat of paint inside and out and some overgrowth in the backyard, the house was ready to be moved into.

"What do you think?" he asked Keiko on the ride to the realtor's office.

"It's a beautiful old house. I can see why you'd want to live there."

*Why I want* you *to live there with me?* "I plan to put a bid on it as soon as we get to the office. Do you think I'm crazy?"

"You'd be crazy not to. Your friend is offering you

an extremely good deal. The house is everything you're looking for and it's close to your family."

"Do you like it?"

Her expression seemed a little taken aback, but he had the feeling she knew deep down why he was asking for her opinion of the house. Yet she only said, "It really is perfect, Marcus. It has so many possibilities."

That was what he wanted to hear—enough for now anyway. An hour later, they were at the bank to start the process of getting a home loan. Then they headed to La Crosse to visit his mother, both of them talking about plans for the house. He shouldn't have been surprised when his sisters and sisters-in-law all but kidnapped Keiko after their visit with his mother, whisking her off to lunch with them. He went with his brothers and got a third-degree teasing, something he expected. He didn't deny the truth when they outright asked him—Keiko *was* pivotal to his future.

He and Keiko met up again at the hospital later, and they ran the rest of their errands together— getting cell phones and looking at gently used vehicles. Neither of them made a final decision on the purchase of a car. Marc's mind was too much on the thought of securing the house, and Keiko admitted on the way back to his father's house that she wanted to see it again, too.

Will had already given him the key, though they were nowhere near to finalizing the sale, and Marc was glad. After touring the inside on their own, he and Keiko walked in the backyard, discussing landscaping possibilities. Since the women had brought her back to the hospital, she'd seemed slightly subdued but insisted she was ecstatically happy and loved his sisters. "Except Jordan, I've never felt so close to other women as I do to your family. They just accepted me from the first time we met and..." She blinked back tears that made him hug her tightly to him. "I can't imagine not having them in my life now. In ways, I'm already closer to your sisters and sisters-in-law than I am to my own sister. She was born when I was in school full-time, just a few years before I went to the States through the foreign exchange program. I think my mother missed being a full-time mother. But Yumako and I have never been close. She's so different. She's... I don't know. Yumako is what most young Japanese girls are these days—all about fashion and money and a cushy life. She came to visit Haruki and me once, when I first came to the Children's Christian Mission Hospital."

Marc nodded. "I think I remember that."

Keiko grinned teasingly. "How could you forget? She came on to you."

"Not really."

"In any case, we told her about Christ that evening...but she wanted nothing to do with Him. She specifically said she wouldn't get involved with an organization that furthered Christianity. Religion is optional in her life, and she likes it that way, but she believes only the Japanese way is right. Haruki and I fully expected her to rush back and tell our parents everything. I still can't believe she didn't."

Marc realized that Keiko must have lived in terror of just what she'd told him before—that her parents would force her to come home and marry Ryu if they knew she was 'forsaking the Japanese way.'

Their arms wrapped around each other, they walked in silence among the budding trees and four-inches-too-high grass. Keiko got excited suddenly while examining the leaves of a white birch tree. "Look at this, Marcus. These are the eggs of a Saturniidae moth—a Luna. I used to raise moths when I was little and as a teenager. Luna's are my favorite. They're giant. So beautiful. Their wingspan is about five inches. They only live four or five days after their transformation. They breed to live—only to accomplish their purpose. They live their whole lives in mere days and yet they manage to carry on the species in that short a time. Isn't that amazing? To have a full, wonderful life filled with purpose, even if it doesn't last long?"

Her last sentence sounded wistful and uncertain to Marc. But she murmured, "Do you have a paper bag or an oversized jar? I'm going to take these and raise them. We can watch them emerge together. I think you'll find it fascinating."

Marc wondered if she was thinking about her own life. Did she feel her life didn't have purpose—the one the Lord meant it to have? Her faith hadn't been tested any more than her brother's had—neither had had the strength to stand up for what they believed in, especially after they'd tried and failed with their younger sister. Maybe they hadn't transformed fully yet and so hadn't learned their true purpose. It had to be terrifying to wonder if they ever would. But Marc knew the time would come for both of them. *I can't bear the thought of losing her if she waffles in her convictions, Lord. Keep her strong in her faith. Give her the strength to stand strong and carry out her purpose as a transformed creature in Christ.*

Maybe it was wrong, but he also couldn't help wishing *he* could be an incentive for Keiko to make her stand and fulfill her purpose. True, everything was going impossibly fast in his life—in hers—right now, but for the first time in a long time, everything happening to him felt right. Everything he'd ever wanted seemed within reach. The prospect of what could happen was something to get excited about instead of dreading.

He waited until she'd carefully removed the egg-laden leaf and placed it into the paper bag, then took her hand. She looked up at him and smiled.

"Will you stay for dinner?"

"I'd love that. I'll have to call Jordan. I'm not ready to go back yet."

"I talked to Josh about you staying with them, and he was totally on board but wanted to discuss it with Justine first. I'll let you know what they decide."

She nodded.

"We can go see my mother before I drop you off. She insists she's not worried about the surgery in the morning..."

"But you want to spend all the time you can with her before. I want to, too."

Normally, he was rarely optimistic, but so much had been going right today. Keiko allowed every touch, every kiss. The chance of getting the house was promising. The future looked too bright for him not to feel confident that his mother would pull through her surgery with flying colors in the morning. He refused to consider any other option.

## Chapter 9

Even as Keiko tried to stay in the moment with Marcus, her mind wandered to her younger sister—so vastly different from the Samuels' females. Yumako would never think to question their parents. Though Keiko didn't know for sure if a husband had been secured for her through *omiai*, she didn't doubt that Yumako had become a school teacher as a way to bide her time until a rich, prominent man married her. Until that time, she lived at home almost entirely on their parents' generosity, a woman in her late twenties. Keiko had once heard the situation referred to as "parasite single" and her sister fit the profile.

"Do you mind if I stay out here in the car? I feel compelled to call my sister. I'm not sure why," Keiko said when she and Marcus arrived at the grocery store to pick up a few things for dinner. "I thought I'd try out my new cell phone."

"And you probably want a little privacy," he guessed.

She smiled sheepishly. He dropped a lingering, tender, sweet kiss on her mouth, and she would have paid every cent in her savings to get it to last a few minutes longer.

"I'll be back in about twenty," he murmured huskily.

She didn't stop watching him until the sliding double doors of the market slid closed behind him and she couldn't see his gloriously strong body anymore. Even she knew she'd become obsessed overnight. She loved watching him move, his limbs loose, limber, rolling in a sexy ramble. He rarely hurried anywhere.

How was it she'd never noticed that before? How was it she'd never noticed how well his clothes fit him, how hot and hard his skin was stretched over his bones? How sensitive that glorious skin was beneath her fingertips? And when he touched her, kissed her, she was instantly lost and so unbelievably needy, she could truly believe he'd woken her from an unceasing slumber she'd been in since birth.

Her head still caught up in the mist of her all-consuming passion for one amazing man, she eased out her phone and dialed the number that had already been programmed into it because she'd taken the memory disk from her old WMMO cell phone. It wasn't until the phone was already ringing that she realized she was calling her sister in the early morning in Japan. Yumako answered, sounding still asleep.

"Goodness. What time is it there?"

"Keiko, are you crazy?" her sister grunted in rapid Japanese.

"I'm sorry. I was thinking of you, so I decided to call. I wasn't paying attention to the time."

"Well, I'm awake now. What is it?"

"I was just..." Before she could gather her thoughts, she found herself asking Yumako if their parents had arranged a marriage for her. She was horrified once the words were out.

"No. They say they haven't found anyone appropriate. I'm not as lucky as you are."

"How can you say that?" Keiko asked in surprise. "Ryu is a leader in the pornography industry."

"What does that have to do with anything? He's meeting a demand. Any good businessman does the same. Or are you worried about the rumors? That he's sick with some infectious disease? Doesn't that make your union more appealing? He won't want to consummate. You can get what you need anywhere else. He's dying. He's filthy rich—he's sure to keep you in fashion until he croaks. And then once he's gone, you can do whatever you want with his...*your* big bucks."

Keiko supposed she shouldn't have been surprised by the cold, selfish words. She'd often thought her sister cared for nothing beyond tradition and the all-powerful god of fashion and luxury she worshipped. Their mother and grandmother had spoiled her right from the start. Whatever she'd wanted, she'd gotten with barely a tantrum.

"I don't care to marry Ryu, Yumako—no matter how rich he is. I would do anything to avoid that."

"Let me guess: The Western doctor? And your Christianity?"

Keiko swallowed, realizing she was setting things in motion that she didn't want to think about, let alone discuss and make absolute decisions concerning.

"You made a promise, Keiko. You'll bring your family dishonor if you even think about getting out of your duty. Is that what you want? To make us all look bad? For what? Love? Faith?"

Was Yumako right? Keiko had accepted her fate when she was just a child. Did that mean there was no escape from it? *Does that mean I can never be with Marcus? But what if we* could *be together? What if...* Keiko swallowed the lump in her throat after her sister said she was tired and was going back to sleep. She didn't bother to say goodbye or good night.

Would Yumako break her promise and tell their parents what was going on behind their backs? She hadn't in all the time since she'd visited them in Nagasaki. *Am I getting as superstitious as Marcus, anticipating the worst because of my own fears?*

Keiko felt as if she'd been riding a merry-go-round, maintaining her equilibrium because nothing had happened to interrupt the ride she'd jumped on in mid-stream. What would happen if the speed picked up or slowed to a crawl? Would everything change, or would she stand firm in her choices? She didn't even know herself what she would do in the face of adversity or persecution. Would she persevere or would her life go spinning out of her control, throwing her into a tailspin? Above all, she didn't want to be tested because she believed she would be found wanting. That would mean she wasn't the godly woman she wanted to be, the woman Marcus needed and deserved.

Marc walked through the supermarket aisles dropping various items into the basket. His father obviously hadn't done any shopping since his wife had gone into the hospital. *Dad's not doing well—he's assuming the worst the way I tend to. My brothers let me know at lunch how much weight he's lost over this whole thing. What would it be like to have the woman you loved ill like Mom is? I can't imagine. Pete lost his first wife, and though he's remarried now and having more children with Kim, he'll never completely get over the loss of Lydia.*

While the thought of slowing things down in his own life—Keiko, the house, getting a car, future career plans—had kept him sane these past few days, he realized his family needed him. Of course he realized that, but he'd been so focused on getting home, nothing going wrong to impede his exodus from Japan, he had to admit he hadn't been as sensitive as he should have been with his father. Tomorrow, those four-plus hours his mother would be in surgery would be excruciatingly hard on his dad. He needed to make himself available, since after all, he was a doctor and could give reassurances that he knew his father had relied on since he'd gotten home.

*Mom seems on top of the world—and I think a big part of that is that she's been worried about me for a long time. Worried that I wouldn't find someone to settle down and have a family with. To my family, to me, that's the other half of the equation—Christ as the head, family coming in a very close second. Now Mom sees Keiko as the answer to her prayers. And I can only hope at this point that things will work out the way I've never even let myself dream they might.*

He wondered how things were going out in the car with Keiko talking to her sister. He knew she wasn't close to Yumako, but she did feel very protective of her. What had she needed to talk to her about so urgently? Because Keiko's words had seemed urgent to him. She'd been slightly withdrawn since lunch with his sisters and sisters-in-law. He wondered if something had happened, something that made her think of her younger sister.

All the women in Marc's family were assuming that he and Keiko were together. *I wish I could have claimed we were. My brothers and brothers-in-law jumped to that conclusion, too. They love Keiko and think she's perfect for me—and they all claimed they'd seen "the way she looks at" me. Not one of them believe her arranged marriage is of any consequence either. That's the American way. Freedom all the way, baby. "If you pursue, she'll let you catch her. End of story" seemed the way everyone saw it. If only.*

No, Marc was sure he wouldn't have any problems getting his family to embrace Keiko unequivocally— they already had. But he was well aware that he wouldn't have it so easy with her family, not even with her brother. After all their years of friendship and Christian camaraderie, Haruki appeared to be reverting to the old ways. Even he would stand against Marc if Keiko decided to be with him. Regardless, Marc was made of stronger stuff. Whatever it took, whatever he had to do, he would to make Keiko Oichi his own. *And that, my friends, is the end of the story.*

He paid for his groceries, figuring he'd given Keiko enough time to talk with her sister. He found her still in the car, staring straight ahead. When he opened the trunk, she got out to help him load the bags into the vehicle.

"How did it go?" he asked.

"I woke her up. She wasn't too happy. I was so focused, I forgot about the time difference."

"How is she?"

Keiko shook her head. "She's Yumako. Nothing I say or do will change who she is, who she was raised to be."

"Well, don't give up. You never know what'll happen."

"I suppose." But he could tell she didn't believe anything could change her sister.

He rolled the cart into the stall, then moved back to her. "I was thinking we could run over to my storage garage before we go back to the house to start dinner."

"Storage garage?"

"Yeah. When I was in college, I had my own apartment and the stuff I bought for it was too good to get rid of. My parents and family didn't have room to hold on to it for me, so I rented a storage garage. If the pieces are in good condition, I'll save myself a lot of money on furnishings if I get the house."

"I have a lot of great stuff in my apartment, too. Maybe we...*you* can use some of it."

Why did he get the feeling she meant to say "we"—that it hadn't been a slip of the tongue? *We're moving in the same direction. Even if we're not ready to talk about it yet, maybe I have good reason to hope we're both careening recklessly toward the same desire for a mutual future.*

# Chapter 10

"Oh, Marcus, this is perfect!" Keiko said in delight as he carried the fifty-five gallon aquarium up to his bedroom. He'd gotten it from his storage garage, where he'd kept a full selection of furniture in nearly pristine condition. She'd intended to start a nice size jar for raising the Luna moths—when she found one. The aquarium would allow for lots of room once the moths emerged from their cocoons. "This will be like a luxury hotel for them."

"I've never raised moths. This should be interesting."

"It is. It's fascinating. Trust me."

"I do."

He placed the already cleaned aquarium on the desk in the corner of the room. In a handful of minutes, he had it set up. She gently placed the leaf with the moth eggs on the bottom with some of the sticks she'd gathered. She misted the aquarium, then Marcus put the dual tops on tightly.

"The larvae will hatch in a week or so. Then they'll need lots of fresh birch leaves. For three or four weeks, we'll have to bring in clippings every other day or so from the tree. They like a somewhat humid atmosphere so we also need to mist the environment periodically, too, but not too much. We don't want mold to grow. When it looks dry, we can mist. And, of course, we'll have to clean out the frass once we have caterpillars."

When Marcus looked at her with a bit of uncertainty in his expression, she laughed. "Don't worry. I'll help you. It'll be fun. I promise."

Downstairs, they heard a door close and footsteps. "Dad must be home."

They went down, and after greetings all around, Marcus said, "I just got some groceries, Dad, and we were going to make dinner."

His father nodded, looking beyond exhausted. "I thought I'd come home, shower, pack a bag and go back to the hospital."

Keiko expected Marcus to insist that someone else spend the night with his mother, but he seemed to realize as well as she did that nothing would keep his father from being at his wife's bedside tonight, watching over her. But Marcus said nothing about that, instead looking at her and obviously worrying about *her* comfort this night. "We have lots of room, Keiko. Tammy and Sam's room would be comfortable for you if you want to spend the night. Then Marc won't have to run you home tonight."

Pastor Samuels didn't wait for either of them to reply. He started up the stairs, saying he was going to get in the shower. Keiko felt uncomfortable in the aftermath of his generous suggestion. But she felt Marcus glance at her and she couldn't deny him when he agreed, "There is lots of room here."

"I didn't pack anything...but I could just swing by Jordan's in the morning and change my clothes."

They would need a good night's sleep, and she didn't want Marcus to have to run her to Jordan's in La Crosse, come back here, and then return to Jordan's for her in the morning. She really did need a car of her own. As soon as his mother was out of surgery and on the road to recovery, she would have to make getting one a priority.

Together, she and Marcus prepared dinner. By the time his father came back downstairs, his suitcase in tow again—probably freshened— they were setting the table. He thanked them for going to the trouble, sat down with them, but ate almost nothing. Between the two of them, Keiko and Marcus did everything they could to reassure him that the procedure would be fairly routine, and Dr. Hall was highly respected in his field. Even as he accepted their encouragement, his mind was obviously elsewhere. "I need to get back," he said, and neither of them protested. He hugged them both, and Marcus assured him that they would be at the hospital at least an hour before the operation.

"I should call Jordan," Keiko said in the silence that followed his father's departure.

Marcus nodded. "I'll start cleaning up."

Keiko went to the living room to make her call. "Sam is here now," Jordan told her. "Why don't I grab an outfit for you and she can bring it to you on her way home tonight?"

"That would be great. I'd appreciate that."

"So...is Marcus really upset? About his mom's surgery in the morning? Sam is. What would they do without their mother? She's like the glue that holds them all together."

Keiko glanced at Marcus in the next room. His father's worry had stolen into him like a virus, and she knew the reassurances they'd freely given him had done nothing to tamp down on his own. "I do want to be here for him," Keiko murmured, realizing that she and Marcus had distracted themselves so well this week, they hadn't allowed themselves to consider that this surgery wouldn't be anything but a complete success. In the cold light of the morning, Keiko suspected strongly that if anything happened to his mother, Marcus would assume God was punishing him for "fleeing" Japan. He wouldn't want to believe such superstitions of himself, but he was the type of man always open to the Lord's guidance and correction. Maybe he'd become hypersensitive to it.

*I don't want anything to happen to his mother either. For possibly selfish reasons. Because I haven't gotten enough time to get to know her—in person. And I want to know her. I want her to know me. In case...*

She didn't allow herself to finish the thought, but she knew what was in the back of her mind when she returned to the kitchen. As soon as Marcus looked at her, he drew her into his arms and hugged her. "Let's pray. For your mother. For your father. For strength," she murmured.

He met her eyes once more, still holding her close. "I feel like I just want to run away. From anything that could mean that I have to face loss."

Keiko nodded. "I felt the same way today when I called Yumako. I don't want to face anything that means I have to give up my freedom and my faith. But faith requires not running away, even when the worst happens."

He sighed. "You're right. We should pray. Together."

"Did you sleep at all?" Keiko asked in a hushed voice when she sat on the couch next to him, tucking herself against him. To Marc's loving eyes, she looked as soft and sleepy as a kitten. He held her the way he'd been longing to for hours.

In answer to her question, he shrugged. He couldn't exactly say what it was, but something nagged inside him, preventing him from sleep, from ignoring anything but constant prayer for his mother.

"Your father got to you," Keiko whispered.

Marc expelled a pent-up breath. "He's really worried. In the past, he's always been the one reassuring, encouraging, believing the best because, in his mind, it's all "God's will." In other words, one way or another, we'd get through it, regardless of what the Lord chose to do. Now..."

"He seems lost."

"Yes. It bothers me, I guess. I've never seen him like this before."

"The prospect of losing someone who's been your companion for most of your life can't be easy. But there's no reason not to believe the operation won't be a total success. We both know that, Marcus. Perhaps we know it best."

"And we know best what can go wrong."

"And so you can't sleep."

Marc turned his head so he could look down and meet her sympathetic gaze. "I don't know why I'm so worried, Keiko." *Or maybe I do know and I'm afraid if I think it out loud, even in my own head...* He expelled a frustrated sigh. *Superstitious!*

She put her arms around his shoulders and hugged him. "What are you reading?" she asked, inclining her head toward the book on his lap.

"My mother gave me this during our visit yesterday. She said it's more important than ever for me to read this now and to *know* it. I didn't know what she meant until now. Until I read this story in this book about a Christian named Walter Ciszek. He volunteered for service in Soviet Russia after joining a Jesuit mission. He felt called to be a priest, but God kept putting him in places he didn't feel he could serve and he felt betrayed because of this. He approached life assuming he knew God's will for him and then further assuming that God would help him fulfill those endeavors. Instead, he learned to accept God's will wherever and whenever he was called to serve."

"Like your missionary work in Japan." Keiko easily guessed where he was going with the story.

Marc nodded. "That's the part I've had the hardest time with. A part of me believes God doesn't want me to be happy. It's easier for me to accept and even assume that He *wants* me to be miserable. When I made the decision to leave Japan for good, I told you I felt like I was rebelling. Like I was Jonah, running from what felt like the further misery God intended to settle on me. I was done. I figured if He wasn't cool with that, He would chase me down and bring me back where He wanted me. I can't be the only missionary in the world dead set against the situation I knew God wanted to put me in. There must be others who obeyed even if they would have rather had their eyes plucked out than go where God was sending them. Is it so wrong for me to feel this way?"

"You know I don't believe it is wrong, Marcus. Because you felt this way and you still obeyed. That's the point."

He shook his head. Unfortunately, that had never felt like the point to him, even when he'd used it as justification for feeling the way he did. It was too much like Jonah who'd, yes, eventually done what God wanted him to—but not humbly, not graciously because he cared about lost souls or obeying the Lord. He'd only preached to the Ninevites, prompting them to repent, to get God off his back. *Is that what I did? And now I'm so bitter, I'm afraid I'll turn from the Lord because I don't believe I can be his missionary for another second?*

"Somehow my mom knew I felt like this about being in Japan all this time. I don't know how she knew. Maybe she could see it my face whenever I came home, or read between the lines in my e-mails. All my life, she's always known exactly what I'm thinking even when I don't say it out loud. She'd always say God put me on her heart. And I know she asked me to read this book because it would help me see that the Lord doesn't want me to be miserable. He wants me to serve Him wherever I am with a grateful heart, one open to lost souls and His leading. Did I go to Japan of His will or my own? Ultimately, *I* made the choice to go into medical missionary service, signed that contract with WMMO. *I* made the decision to stay as long as I did. But then I blamed God for my own stupidity. I have a lot of stuff to work through. But I know that I decided to go to Japan of my own free will...and I served Him there. He used me during that time, regardless of how miserable I was."

"I think I understand what you're going through for the first time, Marcus, since we came home for good. I didn't realize I was doing it all this time, or at least I wouldn't let myself think about it, but I've been running away for a very long time. I don't have that option anymore. I have to deal with the facts, with reality. I just don't feel ready to face my parents or what they expect of me. I'm not sure I'll ever feel ready for that."

Marc tucked her hand against his heart. "Maybe we can help each other."

She laid her head against his shoulder, murmuring, "Yes. You're the only person who can help me. I think I've known that from the moment I met you."

Because he felt compelled to tell her, in small part,

how massive his feelings had become for her, he said, "That's not the only thing I want with you, Keiko. I do want to help you, but I want so much more."

She looked up at him, her expression clear and undimmed. "Good."

He smiled slightly. "Good? Is that all you've got to say?"

"No. But we have time."

"Is that a promise?"

"Is what a promise?"

"That we have time, Keiko?"

"Yes, that's a promise. You promise me, too."

"We have time. All the time in the world if it means..."

She pressed her finger against his mouth to quiet him, then replaced it with her own lips. In the sweet, sexy kiss she gave him, he knew she'd given him time, promises, maybe even her heart. "Do you want to go see your mom?" she asked softly when she drew back just a hair.

"Would you mind? I know it's only four a.m., but I feel like I need to be there."

"Do we have time to shower?"

He nodded. "Of course."

Within a half hour, using separate bathrooms on different floors, they were both ready. The car ride to the hospital in La Crosse was quiet and contemplative. Keiko sat close to him and held his hand, drawing her thumb in a soothing pattern against his. Her strength radiated into him.

Marc couldn't say he was exactly surprised when they arrived and found his father going for coffee in the hall. "Your sisters are here," he told Marc gruffly.

"Did you sleep at all, Dad?"

His father shrugged. "Your mother is awake if you

want to talk to her. I'll smooth it over with the nurses so they don't hassle you."

As quietly as they could, Marc and Keiko walked down the hall to his mother's room. The lights inside were dimmed, but both Tamara and Samantha were sitting in chairs on opposite sides of their mother, their hands linked in a three-way knot. There was a cot set up in the far corner. None of them spoke when he and Keiko joined the knot. But a few minutes later, Tamara whispered to her baby sister. The two rose, hugged both of them and murmured that they were going to stretch their legs.

His mother smiled when he and Keiko took up vigil on either side of her. She hugged and kissed them both. "Thanks for that book, Mom. How do you always know?"

"You're a good man, and whether or not you've always served the Lord *cheerfully* doesn't change that you've always served Him with the attitude of Jesus: 'Not my will, Father, but Yours be done.'"

"I don't think I've been quite that accommodating, Mom."

"Even if you were, you wouldn't give yourself the credit you deserve."

Marc grinned, shaking his head. "How are you?"

"Tired. But I'll never be able to sleep. Everything's going to be fine. My family and my faith is all I need. I couldn't be more blessed."

Within a few hours, the entire Samuels clan, from the oldest to the youngest, trickled in and filled the waiting room to maximum capacity. While the nurses allowed everyone a short visit—the head RN obviously having a soft spot for them and her patient—before long, preparation for the eight a.m. surgery took precedence. Crammed into the waiting room, the family prayed as a group, holding hands all around. Marc could feel the tension when their champion nurse, Nancy, came to tell them that their angel had been wheeled into the operating room and to expect at least a four-hour wait.

The first hour was the longest, and they encouraged each other continuously. The second hour, many of them slept, unable to resist the pull of the long hours without rest. Marc closed his eyes, enjoying the feel of Keiko's head on his chest, the soft sound of her breathing as she napped.

When Nancy came in next, Marc stood, fully expected a positive report or the "no news is good news" bit. But he was surprised to see she had tears in her eyes. "It happened very suddenly. I'm very sorry to tell you that Irene had a series of heart attacks on the table. Dr. Hall couldn't stabilize her. Our angel has passed on."

The buzz in Marc's ears was getting louder and louder.

Faintly, he heard the RN murmur, "The doctor will be in shortly to talk to all of you."

Until Keiko pushed him down to the chair and urged him to put his head between his knees, Marc didn't realize he was seconds from passing out. Briefly, he saw Keiko go out the door of the waiting room on the heels of the RN. Around him, he barely heard the weeping. He felt someone hug him, but he wasn't stable enough to reciprocate. He wasn't sure how much time had passed before Keiko returned. When she sat next to him and put her arms around him, he grabbed hold of her and held on in a strangling grip. He knew he was hugging her too tightly, but she kept assuring him with, "I'm here." By the watery tone of her voice, he knew she was crying along with him.

## Chapter 11

"Are you sure you'll be all right?" Keiko asked. She'd lost track of how many times she'd asked. She knew she didn't want to be alone and she didn't want to leave Marcus for a second.

"Dad needs me. I don't know how he'll get through this day."

Keiko wasn't sure how *Marcus* would. When the horrific news had come in, she'd understood that he wasn't capable of functioning, but, when he was, he would want to know every detail. So she'd followed the nurse from the waiting room and talked to Dr. Hall privately. Though the surgeon had gone into the waiting room and tried to give as concise an explanation for Irene's death as he could, no one had been able to process the information at that time. Marcus hadn't even asked questions then. But hours later, when the news had sunk at least into the surface, he'd demanded answers and Keiko had been able to give them. Death had happened and no one was to blame. Dr. Hall had done everything possible in his undeniable skill to save Irene, but in the end it hadn't been enough. As a doctor, Marcus realized the risks better than anyone in his family, but that didn't make the outcome any easier to accept.

"I'm so sorry, Marcus."

He'd left the car in park on the curb outside Jordan's house, and she worried how he would get home in the state he was in.

"I lost so many years with her."

"I know. But you got to see her again. You got to say all the things you wanted to." Keiko couldn't help thinking about what had gone unfinished though.

His eyes moist, he nodded. "She'll never see me get married. She'll never meet my children and be the grandmother they'll need."

A twinge of guilt filled her. She'd had no idea what was going to happen before it occurred, but she and Marcus had willingly allowed his mother to believe that they were in love and would spend their lives together. Irene had seemed to *need* to believe that. Or, as Marcus had said often, she seemed to know what would happen between them better than even they could guess.

With a sigh, Marcus hugged her, and Keiko held him tightly. "If you need me..."

He nodded, drawing back to look at her. "I'll call you. Don't worry, honey."

"I can't help it."

"We're getting together Sunday at Tamara's after church. You heard that?"

"Yes." Once she came back from talking to Dr. Hall, she hadn't left his side. "I want to be there."

"Good. We have to make plans. I'll pick you up for church Sunday morning."

She wished she'd gotten a car during the days they'd had before his mother's surgery. "I'm grateful."

"If you want, pack all your things, and maybe you can move in with Josh and Justine on that day, too—if you're ready?"

"Yes. If it's no trouble for anyone."

He shook his head definitively. "It's no trouble. We want you with us when we make plans for the funeral... You're part of the family, Keiko."

Keiko swallowed, holding back fresh tears. If he'd said, "You're a part of *me*," she couldn't have felt more tenderness. Every one of his family members had told her that at some point this day. Why did she feel so strongly that she *was*? She and Marcus weren't together. They'd made no plans whatsoever to be together. *Outside of a few, unspoken promises, outside of forever kisses...*

"Keiko...I know this is a crazy time, and it's only going to get worse, but... I don't want to let go of what we've started."

"What we've started?"

"It's too soon. I know that. My head is a mess right now, and that doesn't help. But...I love you, Keiko. I've loved you for five years. I wouldn't let myself fall in love with you because I thought you were officially engaged to another man. But...there it is. I'm in love with you and I want a future with you. Is that even possible?" He shook his head. "If it's not, don't tell me. I can't take anything else. Not today."

His words were whispered, and she knew his pain was already crushing him. Unsure of what to say that wouldn't hurt him, she stared at him with tears in her eyes.

"Okay. Tell me. Tell me something," he continued a little desperately, dragging her even closer to him.

"I don't want to hurt you. But I do want a future with you, Marcus. I don't know what's going to happen and this *does* feel sudden, but it equally feels like I've waited forever for just this."

"Yes."

"There's too much to discuss, and it needs to wait. But I will wait. I promise."

He breathed deep relief, hugging her again. "Thank you, Keiko. For everything. I don't think I could do any of this without you."

She squeezed him against her, knowing she had to let him go and not wanting to. His father needed him.

Only that forced her to do what she had to.

When she eased back, she stroked his worn face, then leaned forward and kissed him softly. She could see by the expression in his eyes that the gesture was nowhere near enough. But he let her go and she in turn let him go to do what he had to.

Marc and his father embraced for a long time when he got in the house. "Did she know, Dad?" he asked quietly once they moved inside and sat down in a dimly lit living room. Anything brighter would have made him feel exposed to horror, so he understood his father's inclination toward shadows tonight.

"How could she have? No, she simply wanted to be prepared." He shook his head, exhaling. "And I have to go along with her wishes, even when I would rather avoid the whole Santa Claus scene."

Marc gaped at his father. "Santa Claus?"

Stephen inclined his head toward the heirloom box on the coffee table. It hadn't been there when he and Keiko left that morning, so his father had obviously brought it down from the bedroom after getting home a little while ago. Marc easily recognized the box. Only the color and decoration were slightly different from his own. At the age of five, he and his siblings had all received an heirloom box of their own with the explanation that they could fill it with whatever they wanted—whatever was important to them throughout their lives, whatever they wanted to pass on to those they loved when they were gone. Marc understood that this particular box had been his mother's heirloom box. If she didn't make it through the surgery, she'd asked her husband to distribute her family heirlooms to those she loved.

"I'll pass things out Sunday when everyone's here," his father said softly.

*Like Santa Claus at Christmas.* "Ah, Dad, I'm so sorry. I don't want to imagine life without Mom. She was..." Tears pressed hard against his already raw eyes.

"Everything. The glue that held this family together, just as Nancy said. Our angel. Did we appreciate her enough? Did I bring this on with my own sins?"

Not for the first time, Marc realized how much like his father he was. Always doubting himself, wondering if he was doing all that he could and should, assuming God was punishing him personally for some perceived sin when anything went wrong.

Leaning forward with his elbows on his knees, Marc reached across to put a hand on his father's knee. "Dad, she knew we loved her more than anything, and she gave every part of herself to the Lord and to her family. She lived out her faith. Her work here was done. We'll see her again. But we still have things to do in this world. Don't give up. Love her and appreciate her now as much as you ever did. And you did, Dad. You did that every day of your life. She knew it."

Marc accepted the advice was as much for himself as for his father. He realized now in blinding clarity why his mother had asked him to read that book. Because, if he hadn't already seen the error in his thinking, he would have been bitter about his mother's death when it happened. He would have let himself harbor anger at the Lord, as if his mother's death was a reprimand for his decision to leave Japan, leave his missionary work there. He couldn't fall back on that now, no matter how much his tendency was to do just that. Ultimately, his choices had been his own and he had no one to blame but himself when things went awry.

He understood the way he never had fully before that the Lord wasn't interested in punishing him but in getting him to the place where he was open to serving wherever he was. He was in that place now. He'd lost one of the most important people in his life, and he would grieve as much as he could while being grateful for all she'd given him, all they'd been to each other. Right from the start, his life had been rich and blessed because of his mother. In some ways, he could easily dwell on the loss of almost twelve years of his life without her, but even then they'd kept in contact on nearly a daily basis with e-mails, sometimes phone calls, back and forth. His only regret was that she'd never seen him marry or have children of his own. That his wife and children would never get to know her and have her blessing and enriching their lives. *But Keiko did know my mom. I know they were also e-mailing back and forth for years. They got that time to know each other. And Mom loved Keiko as much as Keiko loved her.*

His father nodded, squeezing his hand. With a sigh, Marc sat back. "Was Mom sick before this, Dad?" he asked. "I know you two exercised often with daily walks..."

"She was healthy, just as I told you, son, and she always *seemed* healthy for the most part. You know better than I do that that she took good care of herself, but something was going on inside her that we couldn't see."

"The angina was the only symptom?"

"Yes. And even that was so infrequent, we usually

assumed it was from our walks. She'd relax and everything would be fine again." Stephen fixed him with a hard gaze. "Do you think the surgeon missed something? That he wasn't competent?"

"Dr. Hall is one of the best in his field in this area, Dad. I wasn't trying to pull one over on you when I told you that. What happened had nothing to do with his skill or lack of. Her heart wasn't strong enough. There's nothing anyone could have done."

"If she hadn't had the surgery…"

"She would have had another heart attack that probably would have claimed her life. The surgery was necessary because it was the only thing that could have given her the chance at a longer life." *Ironically, it took her life instead of granting her more of one.*

"Thank you," his father said, as if he'd needed his doctor-son's final reassurance to let go of any worries about her care and the choices made in that vein. "And now… I want to give your mother's gift to you tonight instead of waiting for Sunday. I don't want to embarrass you in front of everyone."

Marc frowned in surprise, not certain where this was going until his father slipped the engagement ring he'd given his wife fifty-one years ago from his pocket. Marc's mother had always worn it with her wedding ring. This morning, she'd taken it off for her surgery. The eighteen-karat white gold ring had a hand-engraved band set with two round side diamonds, a row of pave diamonds on each side, and a round diamond in the center. It was an antique now but still as exquisite and brilliantly polished as Marc imagined it'd been the day his father gave it to the woman he loved.

"Your mother wanted this to go to you especially, since you're the only one left. But I don't know if you and Keiko have talked about marriage yet. If you hadn't, I didn't want to embarrass you or her on Sunday. When you're ready and, if you think she'd like this, you can give it to her."

Marc didn't bother protesting that things hadn't gone anywhere near marriage or commitment between them because he knew he wanted their relationship to follow that direction. "I know this will mean as much to her as it does to me, Dad," he said quietly, brushing away tears. "She's from a different culture, Dad, and sometimes it feels like we're worlds apart. In her family, they believe in arranged marriages. She doesn't love her betrothed, nor does she want to marry him. But she also doesn't feel ready to stand up to her parents and tell them she's a Christian and she can't marry a man who isn't."

For a long, silent moment his father simply looked at him, then he said softly, "And so worlds collide."

"Exactly."

"But she loves you?"

"I... Actually, I don't know. Right now..." He remembered the way she'd kissed him when he dropped her off. "Maybe. Someday."

"Then all of these things will have to be faced and dealt with, each in its turn. All you can do is be there for her and love her. Stand with her when the storm comes. But at the time when she needs you to, son, you'll have to let her go by trusting and believing in her. Ultimately, what she does is her choice and it's her battle to fight. If she comes back to you when it's over, you'll have her for all eternity."

The thought of ever letting Keiko go sounded wrong to him, but he knew his father spoke from experience and wisdom. When the time came, he could only pray the Lord would lead him in the direction he needed to go.

# Chapter 12

Keiko woke Sunday morning with a sense of ethereal disbelief that had carried her through the day before—a day without anything more than Marcus' voice on the phone. Had it happened? Had Marcus and his family lost their beloved angel, the heart of their family? Despite how little time she'd had to get to know Irene Samuels in person, she felt she'd loved her like a mother. She felt she'd been accepted as a daughter.

After a shower, she quickly and efficiently packed. Jordan peeked in the guest bedroom, the baby on her hip. "Are you hungry, sweetie? How are you?"

"Not hungry. I'm fine. I just...want to be there for them."

Jordan nodded, coming to hug her. "She was one of those people no one will forget. I loved her almost as much as my own mom. All those years Sam and I have been friends... You'll tell me when the funeral is?"

"Of course, but Samantha will probably want to tell you."

"True. I can't believe you're leaving already."

"I'm not going far."

Jordan sniffed. "And we'll be seeing each other again soon, I know. But...it feels different this time."

"Why?"

"I don't know. Is there something happening with you? With you and Marcus?"

Keiko turned back to finish her packing. "Maybe."

"I thought so. Good?"

"We'll have to see."

Jordan put a hand on her shoulder. "Don't be

afraid, sweetie. Afraid of what's right, what you know deep down is what the Lord wants for you."

"I do that, don't I?" Keiko said a little sheepishly. "Fear even what I know is right? Doubt what's right in front of my eyes is the truth?"

Jordan grinned. "Yeah. You kind of do. But hopefully love will make you fearless."

When the doorbell rang, Keiko's heart leapt with hope that Marcus had arrived. Jordan handed her Duff, and Keiko took him gratefully while her friend went to answer the door. For a long time, he stared at her necklace in utter fascination, trying to get his chubby fingers around the tiny pendant so he could put it in his mouth. "Morning, sweetie pie. You're just a marshmallow this morning, and I want to eat you up!" Keiko murmured.

Giggling, he kissed her so wetly, his chubby arms stealing around her head, she laughed out loud. "A-o," he cried joyfully.

"That's how Duffy says Keiko," Jordan explained behind them, and Keiko turned with the baby in her arms to see Marcus standing there. Though it was obvious he was exhausted and grieving, she loved every gorgeous part of him, especially the vulnerability he displayed without shame.

Keiko moved to give him a one-armed squeeze, asking how he was. "Hanging in there," he offered. He gave Duffy a tender little poke in his belly, and the little boy giggled once more, already holding his arms out to him. "He's beautiful," he told Jordan.

She smiled. "I know you two have to get going."

He nodded, reluctantly letting her take her child from him. "Is this all?" he asked, bending to pick up Keiko's suitcase and carryall from the bed. After she nodded, they both said their goodbyes. On the way to the car, Marcus put his arm around her back despite all he was carrying. "I missed you yesterday," he told her.

"Is your father all right?"

"Under the circumstances, yes, but I worry about him. Mom was his life...for most of his life."

"They had a beautiful life together."

He nodded as he loaded her luggage into the trunk and closed it. "I'm really glad you'll be right next door for a while. Justine's excited—she's got a room all ready for you."

"Your family is so..." She shook her head, unable to express what she wanted to say. "When we were at the children's mission hospital all those years, I saw how you made a family, but you did that for the patients just as much as for yourself. Your family does the same thing. They make a family and bring others in."

"They already love you, Keiko," he told her. "Almost as much as I do."

"Oh, Marcus..." she started, emotion filling her throat so she felt she was strangling on it.

"You don't need to say anything, honey. I know it's too soon and we have a lot to talk about, a lot to do."

She nodded. When he slipped his arms around her waist and kissed her, the instantaneous passion that flared up between them was almost too intense. She held on to him tightly, letting her love for him flow through her physically, wishing she could do so much more to make him feel better. Feel good.

He smiled turbulently when he drew back. "We better go or we'll be late."

That morning his youngest brother Jay, who lived in Peaceful with his wife, gave the sermon at the family church he pastored. There wasn't a dry eye in the place for much of the message. Everything he said seemed to somehow relate to the death of Irene Samuels and how to deal with a loss so profound even as they rejoiced in her being with the Lord they all loved and served. Keiko was embraced at least a thousand times between the church and Marcus' father's home, and she acknowledged once more that she was falling in love with his family as much as she was with Marcus himself. Never had she felt this overwhelming sense of belonging—even what she'd experienced with the Palunacheks, which had been *life* awakening for her, paled in comparison to this.

His father handed out what he called heirlooms to every single person present, telling them that Irene had wanted each one to have this particular item specially. Keiko wept at the treasures. It wasn't until later, after Justine had shown her the room where she'd be staying in their house, that she realized Marcus hadn't been given an heirloom.

Isaiah, Justine and Joshua's four-year-old son, clung to her leg when Marcus found her in the backyard.

"My father gave me mine Friday night," he told her when she asked. "Are you settled in? Do you think you'll be comfortable with my brother and his wife?"

"I love them," she assured him, bending down slightly to give Isaiah a hug. He grinned up at her shyly, the picture of Joshua when he'd been a boy— Justine had already gotten out the family pictures.

When Keiko looked up again, Marcus had a peculiar, sentimental expression on his face.

"I love seeing you with children, Keiko. You were always a good doctor, but you had a knack for never getting too involved with the patients. You're different now."

"I knew I'd be devastated if I let myself love each

child the way I truly wanted to. You could do that without it destroying you. I've always admired you for that. I don't have that kind of strength. Here...I feel like so much is falling away from me—all the rules and regulations and traditions I felt I had to follow at the hospital because of my family and the other Japanese doctors and nurses and patients there. I feel like I'm allowed to be the person I am only here. I can love all your nieces and nephews and Jordan's little boy without getting hurt in the process—without anyone expecting something from me that's part of my duty to the whole of the culture."

The sympathy in his expression was mingled with empathy—because she knew he'd felt the same way during his years of service. But he'd never had any qualms about shedding that exterior when he came home, the way she still did. If Haruki showed up today, she would instantly feel she had to put on masks and guards to protect him from who she was. Even he expected certain things ingrained in them from their family and culture to be in place. If her parents came here...she would never relax, just as Marcus had never been able to in Japan.

"Do you want children, Keiko?" he asked.

"So much," she murmured with feeling. "That longing seems to be getting worse and worse lately. No surprise, huh? Your family has so many young children."

Marcus scooped Isaiah up in his big, strong arms, and his nephew hugged him like he was trying to pop the head off a dandelion. Marcus only laughed and tickled him. "I don't blame you one bit for that longing. I want kids of my own almost to the point of feeling like I won't survive if I have to wait much longer."

Keiko swallowed the lump that filled her throat,

but it remained...especially when Marcus put his free arm around her, pulled her in to the hug with Isaiah, and kissed her deeply without lingering. With that, he led them into the house, where she knew the funeral preparations were being laid out for Thursday.

Only because so many of his siblings had young children who needed to be put to bed did the family disperse before seven that evening. Keiko had bonded almost immediately with Isaiah and she'd gone to read him his bedtime story before his parents tucked him in. Marc had to admit he was glad to have her so close, especially when his father said he was going to bed and that he was fine when he clearly wasn't.

Uncertainty gnawing at him, Marc started cleaning up after the Sunday potluck. While their father had literally just lost his wife and his grief was completely normal, Marc and his brothers and sisters were worried. When his wife had gone on infrequent trips alone, Stephen had been a basket case for those few days though he'd put on a good face for his children. Marcus' parents had married when they were very young, mere children by today's standards, and Marc and his family wondered if it was possible for him to live without her now. Once the days stretched into weeks, how would he cope with the permanent separation and loneliness without her?

*How will the rest of us get by? Everything will be prefaced "without her." Every first step, every graduation and marriage. Mom was the heart of this family. Even now that she's gone, she'll continue to be that until we can accept her loss. And I can't imagine that happening right now.*

Longing to be with Keiko, he carried the trash out to the built-in bins in the backyard. When he stepped off the back porch and looked out over Josh and Justine's connected backyard, he saw lights on in the upstairs windows of their house. Another light flicked on downstairs. Hopeful that Keiko was nearby, he forced himself to go around the backyard, cleaning up there, too. The evening was surprisingly chilly because of a wind that hadn't been present most of the day. Even after he'd tidied the backyard, he lingered, eager for Keiko to come out.

They'd both had a long, emotional day. He knew she was probably as exhausted as he was. Grimacing in regret, he turned and went into the house. He left the backyard lights on, just in case, then continued his clean-up in the living room and sunroom. He'd just returned to the kitchen with trash when he heard a tap on the back door. Without concern, he dropped the bag on the table and rushed to open the door.

"Is it too late?" Keiko asked. "I wasn't sure."

"Come in. Dad went to bed. I was hoping you'd come over."

She smiled, he closed the door once she was inside, and he went to get the trash he'd abandoned, then he washed his hands. "How's everything over there?" he asked.

"Good. Just as I finished reading to Isaiah, he asked where his 'Gran' had been all day. Joshua and Justine handled it, but..." She shook her head with tears in her eyes. "He doesn't understand."

Marc put an arm around her and led her to the living room sofa.

She took a deep breath. "How are you? How's your father?"

He shook his head. "I don't know. Right now, we have to expect that he's not going to feel any better than any of us do. But I don't know how he'll get through this. We all fear he'll do that thing that happens so often with couples who've been together so long. That he'll just waste away."

"We have to do something to prevent that."

"And we'll try, but I have the feeling he won't make it easy for us. He's already urging us to let go of him—in not so many words."

Keiko sighed, turning slightly to lay her head on his shoulder. For a moment, neither of them spoke, then she murmured, "Haruki called. Just after I left Isaiah with his parents."

"Really? What did he say?"

"That he's talked to our parents and they asked about me. I have the feeling Yumako said something to them. That's why they contacted Haruki. They don't usually call us. We contact them when we feel like it. It's the way it's always been. I think Yumako may have mentioned I'm in the States again. When Haruki talked to them, they asked how long I planned to stay."

Marc nodded. "It does sound like they had some foreknowledge."

"Yes. Exactly. Haruki tried to smooth it over, make it sound like there was no cause for concern, but I can tell he believes they're not content to accept that pacification this time. Yumako must have said something."

"About the fact that you and Haruki are Christians?"

Keiko lifted her head, her eyes meeting his. "No. Actually, I think she mentioned you."

"Me?"

She swallowed with obvious difficulty.

"Keiko..."

"I think she told them what I said about not wanting to marry Ryu. They made the rest of the connections, and assumed the reason I don't want to marry him is you."

Marc nodded, understanding her fears clearly now. "Do you still feel it's your duty to your family to marry a man you could never love, could never even respect?" he asked softly.

"I don't know anymore. It's not my way to stand against my family..."

"Wouldn't you much rather be with a man who shares your beliefs, who wants to make you happy, who wants to fulfill all your needs?"

"Of course!"

Marc felt an urgency that he couldn't explain. He'd lost so much. He wouldn't lose Keiko. He refused. "What would your parents do if you told them you were already married, Keiko?"

She blinked in surprise. "*Already* married? What do you mean?"

"I mean, if you were married already, wouldn't the issue of whether or not you're bound to someone you were betrothed to but not officially... I mean, wouldn't the issue be moot if you were already married to someone else?"

Her expression had altered slightly, as if she realized something—wondered specifically where he was going with his questions; as if, maybe, she already knew and felt some hope instead of dread at his upcoming proposal. The perceived hope he saw in her face gave him courage to go ahead with the stirring desire that had become entwined with his heart lately.

"Look, I know we've only been friends, the best of friends, all these years. It's never been more than that, but you have to know why it wasn't more. Because I thought your engagement was more than a simple agreement you made when you were just a kid. That's the only reason I didn't pursue you, Keiko. I wouldn't let myself fall in love with you because you belonged to someone else. But you really don't belong to him, do you? You don't want to. You're my best friend and I love you. I've fallen in love with you, and you're the only woman I can imagine spending the rest of my life with. You're everything I've ever wanted in the woman I want to be with forever. I never want to be away from you. I never want to lose you." He shook his head, not sure what he was saying anymore, or if she was still with him in his hopes. "I know this is fast, but to me it seems like I've waited an endless lifetime for you, exactly you. I don't think anything that happens between us at this point could be fast *enough* for me."

She was staring at him with her mouth slightly open in shock.

"Say something," he begged.

"Are...are you saying you want to...to *date*?"

Marc couldn't help laughing. "Date, yes! I want to be with you. Romantically. I want to kiss you and hold you and... And, maybe it's crazy, but don't you feel like we're meant to be together, Keiko? Please tell me you feel all that's exploding inside me."

She surprised him when she didn't tease him or giggle helplessly at his silly words. Instead, she whispered, "I do."

He closed his eyes as relief settled over him like a soft, cozy blanket. "We could be together forever—all the time, night and day—if you married me. And you wouldn't have to be forced into a marriage you don't want with a man who disgusts you."

She'd put a shocked hand over her mouth at the

words "if you married me." She looked both terrified and intrigued.

"There's no rush, Keiko. We can take our time, but..."

She shook her head. "We *don't* have time."

"We don't?"

"Not if what Haruki believes will happen does come to pass. But..." She grasped the front of his shirt lightly. "That's not the reason. It feels fast, but it also feels like I've waited all my life for you, too. I feel the same about you. I'm scared about the prospect of confronting my parents, but my heart is for you. I know it is. I've known the truth of that since the first time I met you, even when I wouldn't let myself accept it."

"You want to date...and..."

"...get married," she finished. "Yes. I want to marry you more than anything, Marc. Soon. Maybe we could..."

"What?" he demanded.

"No. Tonight, maybe we can just enjoy the kissing part."

He couldn't help laughing, but then he was holding her, she was holding him, and their lips were meeting and rejoicing in all that they were to each other and all that they would be. Marc drew back to get his mother's engagement ring. "My father gave me this as Mom's heirloom present to me. To us."

"Oh, Marcus, it's so lovely." Her eyes adored the ring and its implications. "Is this wrong?"

"She wanted us to have it. She wanted to see us together more than anything."

Keiko nodded. "She did. I know she did."

When he slipped the ring on her, finding it slightly too big, she looked at the brilliance in the light.

"We can get it fitted tomorrow."

"It's so beautiful, Marcus. Are we really doing this?"

"You tell me. Whatever you want. As soon as you want."

She smiled softly up at him. "I love you. I want to be with you as soon as possible...just as your mother would have wanted."

## Chapter 13

Justine said nothing the next morning, but Keiko knew she saw the familiar engagement ring at breakfast. She gave Keiko a hug that spoke volumes. "You couldn't be more welcome in our family, Keiko. We love you." She drew back smiling. "Are you sure you're okay taking Isaiah today?" She sat down again and added more cooled French toast to her son's plate.

"Marcus and I are looking forward to the adventure. Please don't worry."

Justine chuckled. "I'm not worried. He'll be in good hands. And it'll be good practice for the two of you."

Keiko didn't get a chance to comment on that little nugget of instigation. Joshua walked into the room and dropped kisses on all of their heads. Keiko and Justine shared a smile.

"How did it go? Last night...when I went out of the room?" Keiko asked in a veiled way. Isaiah was too young to truly understand death and that he wouldn't see his beloved grandmother again until he got to heaven.

"He cried," Justine said softly, her eyes reddening. "He understands...but doesn't, if you know what I mean."

Keiko nodded. After breakfast, she insisted on cleaning up the kitchen and Isaiah, shooing Joshua and Justine off to work. She enjoyed the tasks, but she was eager to go next door. Marc was waiting and pulled her into an embrace. At their feet, Isaiah hugged their legs.

"Are we still going forward with what we talked about last night?" he asked when the boy rushed off to the toy box in the living room.

"I want to. Do you?"

He chuckled. "I did some research last night—because we've both been out of the country for so long, despite still keeping up our citizenship. We have to have been living in Wisconsin for the last thirty days in order to apply for a marriage license. Then there's a mandatory five-day waiting period once we apply. So, taking into account the almost week we've been here, the soonest we could get married is the end of next month."

"I want to check in with my Immigration Service Officer, though I just talked to him when we arrived. I made an appointment then just to make sure everything has been kept up, so I can discuss this with him during that meeting. It's this Wednesday—in the morning. The office is in Minnesota. Will you come with me?"

"Definitely." Marc squeezed her tightly again. "I'm glad you kept your permanent residency up. It'll save us a lot of time."

"Don't forget headaches." Keiko laughed, remembering how long it'd taken for her to get all the paperwork, etc. processed in the first place. At times, she'd felt the Immigration officer was inventing hoops for her to jump through.

From the living room Isaiah asked about his grandfather, and Marc said, "He went for a walk this morning, buddy."

"How is he?" Keiko asked, seeing the trace of worry in Marc's eyes.

"As well as can be expected, I guess. He made a point of insisting that I go out and do whatever I need to today and not to worry about him."

"Are you going to?"

"Yes—unfortunately, we have a lot to do. But I'd

like to check up on him often, especially during lunch."

Keiko nodded. "Isaiah will need a nap after lunch anyway. That works perfectly. So, what do we all have to do today?"

"Getting the ring adjusted. Cars."

"Yes. That's top of the list."

"I have a meeting at the bank to fill out paperwork for the home loan..."

Keiko realized she'd almost forgotten that he was buying his friend Will's house next door. It felt like all that had happened so long ago.

"Do you really like the house, Keiko? Is it something you can see us living in together?"

"Yes. I loved it from the first time I saw it. It's perfect. Everything we could ask for when we start our new life together."

"I admit I was thinking of both of us whenever we looked at it. I could only see us together there. Did you, too?"

She nodded, remembering how she'd thought her living room furniture in her Chicago apartment would fit so well in the living room of the house. In some ways, it was as if they'd begun planning their lives together before they left Japan. *Actually, it's as if I've planned my life around Marcus even before we met. Everything about the life we're now openly planning together feels right, even meant to be. When I prayed last night before bed, I could feel the Lord's hand on me, just as when Marcus and I prayed before I went next door. Marcus said he felt rightness, too...along with his usual superstitions about wanting to hurry because he irrationally feels he's going to lose me if there are any delays. He must have felt that way when he found out we have to be living in the country and this state for thirty days before we can apply for a license.*

Most of the morning was taken up with both of them purchasing like-new cars from the dealership they'd investigated last week—they both decided on the same conservative, efficient make and model. The only difference was in the colors they chose. His was black, hers white. Isaiah loved the game room in the dealership, and Keiko and Marcus had no trouble keeping an eye on him there and making sure he was happy.

They drove their new cars home, then made lunch. Stephen joined them and Keiko was pleased to see how well he interacted with his grandson despite the obvious pain he was in. Grandfather and grandson both took naps after the meal, and Marcus kissed her downstairs, saying he had to run to make the appointment at the bank. "I'll be back in an hour."

"Isaiah should be awake then."

"I'd like to run over to the County Clerk's office in La Crosse today—just to make sure we're set up for applying for our marriage license. Once we talk to them there, we can plan our wedding date."

The words were beyond exhilarating, and Marcus kissed her again with the kind of passion that made her blush even as she cherished the intimacy ahead of them. Never in her life had she expected to have a relationship like this. Any trepidation she felt about the unknown was overshadowed by her excitement for the future. She knew if she kept her focus on Marcus and their life together, nothing could steal her happiness.

"When will we tell your family?" she asked softly. "I think Justine already knows."

"The funeral is on Thursday," Marcus said, and Keiko embraced him a little tighter. "Let's hold off until after that. How about Friday? We've already been invited to couples' night at The Pier with my brothers and sisters. I don't know if they'll still want to do that, but if they do, it would be a good time for our announcement."

She nodded, smiling. The weekly get-together included all of Marc's sisters and brothers and their spouses. She and Marcus had been informed about attending it together almost from their arrival in the States.

"I think we should tell my dad as soon as possible. At dinner tonight?"

"Yes. I think he would like that."

Marcus kissed her once more, then left for his appointment at the bank. Keiko couldn't help thinking, *When will we tell* my *family?* The mere thought made her blood feel like ice freezing her veins. If her parents knew, they would try to put a stop to it. Better that they be told after the fact, even if it meant none of her family would be there for the happiest day of her life.

Knowing that if he said they had something to tell him he couldn't refuse, Marc managed to coax his father into the kitchen while he and Keiko made dinner that evening. Before they could say anything, he heard a familiar beeping. He set down the veggie-filled salads they were planning to eat while waiting for the chicken dish to finish baking. Shaking his head, he said, "I still haven't had time to get my cell phone set up properly. All my calls have been going straight to voice mail and I don't recognize the beeping to tell me I have a message."

He got his phone from the pocket of his jacket and

pressed the button to call up his voice mail. After he entered the code, he listened to the message from the loan officer he'd been meeting with about the house. The call must have come in hours ago. He'd completed the application process there after lunch to see if he could afford the house. As he listened, he expected to hear that there was a problem with the application. The loan officer had been impressed with Marc's more than adequate down payment, but he'd confided that approval could be delayed or even denied because of the fact that Marc had been out of the country for twelve years. While he had an excellent history of paying his bills on time and making monthly deposits in his account, he had no credit to show for himself during those years. However, the message from the loan officer told him that, just as with the purchase of his car, that situation really wasn't a great impediment.

"I can't believe it went through so fast."

"It's a small town," his father said on a shrug. "And you're low-risk. You're a doctor and you don't have any debts."

There were a lot of things to think about— inspections and titles and insurance, not to mention all the closing details. *And a funeral and a wedding in there. I need to get back to work eventually...and that'll require a thousand decisions.* Initially, Marc had considered the multitude of tasks helpful in keeping his mind off his recent loss. But the thought of everything he had to do settled on him in a sudden, heavy dump. He sat down at the kitchen table, placing his phone next to him.

"Do you want me to set your phone up to receive calls as they come in instead of having them go directly to your voice mail box?" Keiko asked.

He nodded, grateful for one less task. In a minute, she had it fixed. Marc couldn't explain what he was feeling even to himself, but he tried to shake himself out of it as they discussed when the closing date might be, when he might move in to his new home.

"I have to consider moving as well," his father murmured.

"Moving? Why would you have to move, Dad?"

"This house is the church parish. After I retired as the pastor of the church, an interim pastor came and it was decided that your mother and I would remain here in the parish. Jay made that same decision when he took over pastoring the church recently. But this house is too big for just me. And Jay and Ashley are planning to start a family that will grow. In the coming years, they'll need more space than the apartment they've been living in gives them."

"Where will you go?" Keiko asked.

He shook his head. "I don't need more than a small apartment. That would be adequate for my needs. And I know your sisters and my son's wives, Marc. I won't need a kitchen of my own. They'll make sure of that."

Keiko laughed, but Marc didn't like that his father was giving up what that had meant so much to him and Mom. "Dad...I'm sure Jay and Ashley wouldn't mind if you stayed here in the parish—"

"No. I wouldn't do that to them. They're a new family. Newlyweds. They need their own space. It would be better for all involved if I got an apartment. I'll be fine. There's nothing for any of you to worry about. I can take care of myself. I haven't had to for a long time, but I'm certainly capable of it."

Marc couldn't help his thoughts. His mother had just died. It was too soon to be considering such a major change. *Just as "too soon" as it is for me to be thinking about getting married in a month, buying my own house, and starting my career in a new direction? And then there's my desire to start a family ASAP... When am I supposed to grieve with all this stuff going on? Or was that my point in setting so much in motion? To avoid grief?* It'd been working, too.

"The two of you had something to tell me..." his father hinted pointedly.

The oven timer went off, and both Marc and Keiko rose instantly. Neither of them protested that they would get it. They went together. "Are you all right?" she whispered when they reached the timer. "Do you want to wait?"

How did she always read his mind? He couldn't help marveling about that, even as he wondered if they *should* wait. But he couldn't regret asking Keiko to marry him. Everything was happening too fast, too much was happening at the same time, yes. Still, he'd waited his whole life for these very things. He wasn't willing to put any of them off, despite the timing. *Mom above all would have wanted me to have these things. She knew best what I gave up to surrender my life to the Lord's work.*

Marc put a hand on Keiko's arm and squeezed lightly. "No. Let's not wait another minute."

Together, they got the chicken casserole, plates and utensils. When they were sitting again, Keiko insisted on serving them. Marc's father was looking across the table at both of them expectantly. As soon as she was done and sat beside him on the bench, Marc put an arm around her. "Dad, Keiko and I are engaged. Did you already know that?"

His father reached across the table for Keiko's hand, saw the engagement ring—his wife's—that fit her so perfectly. He looked up at them, smiling and nodding. "I suspected..." His voice cracked. "She would have wanted this. She waited a long time to see you happy with the woman the Lord intended for you, Marcus. Your engagement couldn't have come at a better time."

Seeing the tears in his father's eyes, Marc couldn't hold back his own. His thoughts had been the opposite. He hadn't been sure the engagement was good timing. Even now, he felt uncertain about that. But they all rose and hugged and celebrated. Dinner was a watery affair, and Marc forced a levity he didn't feel because they needed it and each seemed to realize how much they did.

Still, as soon as they'd finished eating and his father insisted and would brook no argument on cleaning up, Marc felt overwhelmed with the grief he realized now he hadn't allowed himself to experience. He'd been in a strange holding pattern for the past few days, since the unexpected had happened and his mother had gone on to be with the Lord.

Although he excused himself and went to his room, he kept the door open. Keiko followed, as he'd known she would. She put her arms around him and held him close, her face pressed to his chest. "I know," she whispered, her tears mingling with his when he bent to put his cheek to hers. "I kept thinking the same thing. It's not right. She should be here. She wanted this as much as we do."

"I dated a lot of women when I was younger," he murmured.

Laughing in shock, she pulled back and looked at him. "Did you now?"

"I admit it. I did. I've spent a lifetime looking for my Mrs. Right. When I brought one home, my mother would always treat her with respect and kindness. She didn't say the truth unless I asked for it—and I always did. But she knew none of those girls were for me. As soon as she met you, almost six thousand miles away, she knew you were the one. You saw that, too, didn't you? Saw that my mother loved you like a daughter from that moment?"

"Yes."

"It's not enough, it's not fair, but I know this is right, Keiko. No one would have been happier about this than my mother."

"No one except us."

He nodded, sighing as they settled back together. "Everything suddenly feels crazy, like it's spinning out of control."

"I feel that way, too, except here...when we're together, in each other's arms."

"You ground me, too. As soon as I see your face, as soon as I touch you, I know we're doing the right thing. Tell me again you love me, Keiko."

She didn't hesitate. "I love you."

"Then nothing else matters. We'll get through this. Even if it's hard, we'll come out stronger."

## Chapter 14

"This is just like your mother's heirloom box," Keiko said in surprise when Marcus set the large chest on the bed. "Other than the color."

He nodded. "Everyone in my family has one."

She sat down and looked inside, picking up photographs and items that he'd treasured enough to put in his keepsake box. She gasped when she saw a familiar item. As she lifted the obviously empty box, she murmured, "*Honmei choco.*" *True feeling chocolate.* A year ago, she'd given Marcus the NIKO chocolate box on Valentine's Day.

He shook his head at her. "You said it was *giri choco.*"

*Obligation chocolate.* Yes, she'd seen no way to do anything else but call it that. In Japan, women giving men chocolate on Valentine's Day was customary, and every male in her life had been given the *giri choco.* Last year, when she'd been making her purchases, she'd realized she didn't want to give Marcus the courtesy chocolate the rest of the males she knew would be receiving. Instead, in private, she'd given Marcus this expensive box of fine chocolates and called it obligation chocolate.

"I couldn't tell you it was sweetheart chocolate. I wouldn't let myself believe it was," she admitted now.

A month later, on White Day, when men reciprocated to the women in their lives, Marcus had given her Vosges Haut-Chocolat. Neither of them had spoken of what they'd done. She'd recognized the expense he'd gone to, yet he hadn't said or done anything to imply it meant more than friendship. But he'd kept the box even after it was empty just as she'd kept hers.

Marcus sat down on the bed next to her and told her about his treasures, rich with tales from his childhood. Once he set the closed treasures back in his closet, he returned and they both settled back against the headboard on the twin bed. "What kind of wedding do you want, Keiko? Something big and fairy-tale like, the way most American women dream of, or a Japanese wedding?"

She shook her head instantly. "Neither. Not a traditional Japanese wedding. That wouldn't be right for us. And nothing like the elaborate event Jordan and Micah had. I want something small. Just immediate family and our closest friends."

Marcus smiled. "That's what I want, too. Did I ever tell you that I performed Jay and Ashley's wedding ceremony—in a parking lot at night under a street lamp?"

She giggled. "I remember you told me the last time we came home, when you married them." She knew Marcus had spent part of his college years entertaining the prospect of becoming a minister and had taken the necessary steps to become ordained in the state— ultimately, he'd changed his mind about his future career but retained the authority to perform marriages.

"Seems fitting that Jay should marry us."

"Not your father?"

Marcus shook his head. "He's given up all things pastor-related. I think Dad would prefer to watch the ceremony, not perform it."

Keiko couldn't argue with him.

He gazed down at her in wonder. "So...something small."

"And conservative. But beautiful."

"You're reading my mind again. How do you do that, my love?"

"I guess the same way you read mine."

He smiled, tracing the lines in the palm of her hand. "I don't want to put everything on you, honey, but getting the house set up is really more my thing. What if you plan the wedding and I get the house ready for us to live in? I think you'll do a great job with the wedding—better than I ever could."

*Planning my wedding. I never thought this day would come—I dreaded it when the groom was someone other than this amazing man.* "Can I enlist your sisters and sisters-in-law?"

"You'll make them happy if you do."

"What do you need to do with the house?"

"Other than painting and giving it a thorough cleaning out? Getting the furniture in place, whipping that backyard into shape again, plotting out a garden. I've always wanted to do that. I'll have to recruit my brothers to help me with some of it."

She smiled. "It sounds like a fair trade to me. What about..." She lowered her eyes to their entwined hands. "...the honeymoon?"

When he urged her to face him, Marcus didn't seem at all embarrassed, the way she was. He smoothed back the hair that fell across her cheek. "What do you want, honey?"

"You don't want to be traveling, do you? Not so soon after returning to your home?"

"Do you want to go somewhere?"

"Actually, I was thinking..."

He turned her toward him, holding her securely, so that she couldn't have looked away from him if she wanted to. "What? Tell me, Keiko. I want what you want."

"Our new home will be everything, more than I can even imagine. A week or two of just us there, nowhere to go, nothing to do..." *Nothing except...* Her entire body warmed at the prospect of all they would do and be to each other, how intimate and perfect their union would be. "That sounds perfect to me."

He smiled softly, obviously loving the idea as much as she did. "I'll have to make sure we don't have anyone dropping by often during that time. I want you to myself for two weeks straight. Actually, I'm not sure two weeks will be anywhere near enough."

"I'm not sure it will be for me either." Keiko felt like she was smothering, unable to draw breath or expel it. The thought of being alone with Marcus, all day, all night, in ways that she'd only considered recently, sent her reeling in pleasurable anticipation.

His breathing sounded as ragged as hers felt as they looked at one another, sharing in that way their newfound longings.

"What about your family, Keiko?" he asked in a hoarse voice that further stimulated her already raw nerve endings. Her own reaction surprised her. *I want him so much. Sometimes I wonder if I can last as long as we have to to be together.* "Haruki and you are close. He's been one of my closest friends for these past twelve years. I would love to have him at our wedding."

The abrupt transition from the warm-caramel arousal stealing through her limbs to ice water panic was more than a little uncomfortable for her. "I... Marcus, you have to understand that knowing we're together has changed Haruki. It's made him...revert in some ways. It's true that he was a Christian and dated other girls while we were growing up in the United

States. He had a crush on Jordan for a long time. Still, he went through with the arranged marriage with Gin that our parents planned when he was eleven— without a formal meeting, since they both agreed to the marriage without it. She isn't a Christian. The two of them didn't know each other at all, nor was there any love between them when they were married. I'm not even sure they love each other now, despite the fact that they have two children together. Gin has no idea that he's a Christian. In ways, she doesn't know the first thing about her own husband."

Marcus frowned. "He never mentioned some of that to me."

"You and Haruki never talked about his marriage?"

"Yes. In particular, I asked him some questions just before we left. I wasn't aware that he never met Gin before the marriage ceremony. What will your parents do if they find out we're getting married? What will Haruki do if they learn the truth?"

Closing inside herself, she sat up, glancing back at him from the edge of the bed. "Please, Marcus, we can't tell them. We can't give them a chance to ...try to stop us."

"You want to wait until it's too late for them to do anything?" he guessed.

They'd discussed this. In her memory, he'd been the one to suggest that they marry and then let the chips fall where they would. He'd been the one to make her see that once the deed was done, her parents couldn't force her to marry Ryu. "Then all they can do is disown me for marrying a round-eye."

He laughed in shocked disbelief. "Round-eye? Well, that's a new one for me. But Keiko, you're a grown woman. There's no legal precedence for a parent disowning a grown child."

She started to explain, but he shook his head, drawing her back to him. "I know. It's about family honor and duty, not legalities."

He sighed, and she snuggled closer to him, her head on his strong chest. "Once we're together, nothing else will matter, Marcus. I promise. Only our love matters."

He nodded. "Okay. You know, one of the things Haruki and I talked about in the past is that your parents never showed physical affection for each other in front of you or in public at all."

"Not even once."

"Haruki told me about Japanese marriage and...I can't accept that way, Keiko. I can't accept any part of it. I want a passionate marriage. I want it to start that way on our wedding night until death do us part. I'll never be less attracted to you than I am now. I'll always want to make love to you. I'm a hundred percent sure of that. If anything, my desire for you will only grow throughout our years together. I don't want to be in a marriage where we aren't free to reach for each other sexually, in ever deepening love. I don't want you to believe that, once we have a child or several children that we can't or shouldn't be together sexually."

She'd never been open about such topics, and she couldn't help her mortification as she pressed her cheek against his chest, her eyes squeezed shut. Yet she admitted, "I want us to be in love, physically and romantically. In all ways, Marcus. I don't want that to stop either. I was raised in the United States. I want what Jordan and Micah have. What all your siblings and their spouses have. I won't settle for less either."

She could feel the sheer volume of the sigh

growing until he exhaled. Needing to ease the tension, she glanced up at him. "If I become fat after I have children, you'll still want me?"

"That's not even possible. I'll love you always, no matter what. And I'll always want to make love with you. I promise."

"It is possible. My cuteness won't last forever."

He chuckled. "Neither will mine. I love dessert and fried foods too much. You can testify to that."

That he did. But she couldn't imagine not wanting him to touch her, not wanting to touch him everywhere and bring him pleasure. She understood what he was saying. In her loving eyes, he would always be the perfect man. Nothing could change that.

"I promise you, Keiko, that my love and passion for you will only grow stronger and deeper all the years we're together."

She nodded. "So will mine. We want exactly the same things, Marcus. We want them together."

"Children?"

"Yes," she said on a half gasp. "Please. Many children."

"How many?"

"At least two. A boy and a girl. We have to keep going until we have at least one of each."

Marcus grinned at her, his arms snaking around her waist and easing her closer, until their bodies all but merged. "I love that idea. As long as it's safe and you're healthy. How soon?"

She could almost feel him holding his breath in anticipation of their mutual desires again. "For me, the sooner the better."

His grin spread across his face. "Really?"

"You want to start trying right away, too, don't you?"

His large hand cradled her hips, stroking up and down until she thought the coil of desire growing inside her would shatter with her needs. "I wouldn't mind spending a few years together as newlyweds who can't keep their hands off each other," he murmured huskily. "But, yes, I've waited a lifetime to start a family of my own. I want that with you more than anything. Neither of us are getting any younger."

Her chances of getting pregnant if they waited would be less. She didn't want to risk that. If they couldn't keep their hands off each other before, during and after she got pregnant, that only made the prospect more appealing.

When he kissed her, his body covering hers on the small bed, Keiko felt swept away like never before. She knew it was because they'd shared their hearts and dreams so completely, the slightest physical intimacy only bonded them more. When he lifted his head and looked down into her face, she could sense how aroused he was—just as she was. Marcus murmured a prayer of gratitude that she added her fervent confirmation to.

She tasted salty tears in his next long, soul-deep kiss, and she reached up to brush the wetness from his face with comforting fingers. He was thinking of the mother he'd lost, the hopes he'd associated with her being there. Keiko felt the loss keenly, in her own way. Having Marcus' mother beside her during all their preparations for their life together would have filled part of the hole created from not having her own mother beside her on the happiest day of her life. She understood that Marcus would experience his own emptiness on that day—one that he wouldn't be able to wish away any more than she could.

The next several days passed in a kind of blur that kept Marc in an emotional overload state. Things were moving forward on his purchase of the house, especially with Keiko insisting on contributing to the down payment. Their monthly payment would be much more affordable than Marc could have imagined when he'd started the process. Will was more than agreeable to speeding up the process—even giving Marc the go-ahead to move in immediately and complete the work he needed to do to make the house ready for his marriage at the end of the month. They'd set a wedding date for Saturday the twenty-first, which was the very day they were legally allowed to get married.

Because of the busy day they would have on Wednesday, Marc and Keiko spent the night in an adjoining hotel room on Tuesday, since her appointment with the Immigration officer was early the next morning. Despite a panic attack that he managed to stave off before it became full-blown, Marc enjoyed the time wooing his bride-to-be. His desire to make love to her had reached a critical juncture and he knew if they weren't both so committed to Christ, they would have given each other everything that evening. It would have been so easy. But Marc had been raised better than that and Keiko deserved to be treated with the respect that saving themselves for their wedding night accorded her.

The next morning, they found out that everything was in line with Keiko's citizenship because she'd made such a diligent point of keeping up on all the requirements for maintaining it. Marc couldn't help being wildly grateful about that. In some ways, that made everything feel meant-to-be because so much simply fell into place for their upcoming union. How long could that last?

His mother's wake took place Wednesday evening and was a precursor to what would be a long couple of days. Marc didn't want to face it but deep down he felt his apprehension growing. He kept expecting something to go wrong—and not something small, like he'd find a termite infestation in the house or the wrong color flowers would be delivered the day of the wedding. He expected something major to destroy everything he and Keiko were building. He had so many doubts that he'd actually begun to wonder if he'd misread the situation. Was he working against the Lord's will? He could no longer tell right from wrong anymore. Inside him were brick walls and dead ends— shored up with anger and grief he didn't want to allow to gain root but couldn't seem to pray away. He wanted a life with Keiko so badly, he could no longer see the situation logically. He had a very strong suspicion that the downfall of their dreams would come from her family—stemming from the fact that Keiko couldn't and wouldn't confront them with her faith and her decisions. Worse, he couldn't get himself to go against her wishes. He didn't want to be the one to tumble this precarious house of cards.

The funeral took place on Thursday, and Marc felt raw with fatigue and emotions sitting square on the precipice of his fragile state of mind. His father had withdrawn more and more, and Marc had let him. He understood that nothing could heal the wound his father was nursing—nothing but time...maybe. The burial happened in a downpour of cold, relentless rain, and the horror of losing his mother came to him then as their large group was pounded by the elements. A million times, the question *why?* reverberated inside his head. That he couldn't answer the one question that hounded him increased his fury at the unfairness of losing his mother just when he had his life back.

Tamara held the reception in her home. Marc wanted nothing more than to return to his parents' house, the one where he'd grown up so happy and contented. He wanted to shut down there.

"Mom was ready," Tamara said in the kitchen when Marc went with her to put more sandwiches on trays and to make another urn of coffee. "I hate even thinking about that, but she's been so close to the Lord all her life." She glanced over at him, looking as tired and red-eyed as he felt. "I thought Dad would go first. I really did. After all that horrible stuff with Samantha a few years ago, I was convinced Dad wouldn't survive it. And now I wonder how he'll get through this."

She was speaking honestly. Her fears were his own. But lately he hadn't felt capable of voicing them with anyone except Keiko. She was his shelter in this storm, his anchor.

Tamara shook her head. "I sometimes wish there was a reason that these things happen. That we could know why. But I don't think there is a reason *per se*. Mom was sick and maybe she had been for years but never knew it. Death is a part of life, and we all have to die eventually. There's nothing more to it than that. But I sometimes wish for someone or something to blame. Isn't that ridiculous?"

Putting an arm around his older sister, Marc shook his head. "No. You've just voiced the universal struggle to understand purpose."

Tamara leaned back against him. "You're not blaming yourself, are you, Marc? You've always tended to do that, just like Dad. Like everything has to happen for a reason and the reason is somehow outside of God's will."

When he didn't say anything, she turned and hugged him. "Don't, Marc. Don't do that. Promise me. You had nothing to do with Mom's death. You're finally back home for good, and we can have you in our lives every single day again. Before this happened, Mom said to me that she'd had a full life, one that was happy and everything she could have wanted for herself. She had no regrets."

"If anyone could claim that, it was her."

Tamara nodded, stepping away to finish setting up the coffee. "We decided to change our weekly dinner at The Pier to a Bible study. Dad asked if we'd help him move into his new apartment in the morning. Then we're helping Jay and Ashley move into the parish in the afternoon. We're considering making our weekly get-together a permanent Bible study on Friday nights, maybe at all of our houses, taking turns. You and Keiko are coming, right?"

Marc's father had mentioned the apartment that morning before they'd left for the church. Marc had just made the decision to move most of his things into Will's house tonight, including his twin bed, which he'd use until he and Keiko picked out their marriage bed. "I'll talk to her. We'd both love that. We'll need it after today."

"Mom and Keiko talked a lot, didn't they? These five years, since she's known you?"

"How did you know that?" Marc asked in surprise. "Did she say something?" Keiko had never even told him whether or not that suspicion he'd had was true.

"Mom talked about her a lot. She always seemed to realize that there was more between the two of you.

She was right, wasn't she?"

How could he deny it? Especially since he and Keiko were planning to tell his family about their engagement tomorrow night. "Mom knew it before we did."

Tamara smiled. "I believe that. And I know why Mom loved her so much. Keiko is perfect for you, Marc. The Lord couldn't have found a more perfect woman for you. The two of you will have the most gorgeous kids someday."

Marc didn't often get embarrassed, but he couldn't help chuckling in shock now. He didn't dare respond—and had the feeling he didn't need to. No one would be surprised once he and Keiko made their announcement tomorrow.

## Chapter 15

Keiko and Marcus made their proclamation just after the informal, brief Bible study. Everyone was tired, looking like they were ready to drop after a day of lifting heavy furniture and boxes, and/or watching scores of children while the others helped with the dual moves. Nevertheless, as soon as the news was out, Keiko found herself surrounded by the women and shepherded into the kitchen supposedly to get dessert and coffee. After fielding at least a million questions, Keiko laughed giddily. "There's so much to do and so little time. I know very little about American weddings—only what I saw with Jordan and Micah's elaborate wedding. Marcus and I want something much less formal—scaled back considerably. I could really use some help on even knowing where to start."

Her words only succeeded in ratcheting up the excitement level among her new sisters. Plans were made for them to get together the following Thursday at Michael's, a cozy little Peaceful restaurant with to-die-for desserts, to begin aggressive preparations. Keiko hugged each one of the women. "I appreciate your help."

"What about your family?" Samantha asked a moment later, once they got around to starting the dessert and coffee tray. "They're coming from Japan, I assume?"

Keiko swallowed. She'd worried this question would come up. "I'm...well, things are different in Japan. My family arranged a marriage for me when I was very young and they wouldn't understand any of this. It seems best to not tell them until later." *When there's nothing they can do to stop it.*

Her sisters looked at her in shock. Surprising her, they were sympathetic. Justine pointed out that women in other countries didn't necessarily have the freedoms American women enjoyed and expected. That in some ways, females were treated like property, not individuals with minds and choices. Keiko hugged her for being so understanding. Not knowing what to expect, she'd been concerned one or more of them might try to insist she invite her family.

"Maybe it is for the best that the two of you wait to tell your family until it's a done deal," Justine said.

"Thank you. This isn't an easy decision. I wish my family could be there, especially my brother and my..." She swallowed heavily, trying not to remember the times she'd played *"san-san-kudo,"* as a little girl. Her grandmother had let her wear the *Tsuno Kakushi* bridal hood while her mother made up her face so she could pretend to perform the ceremony of three-times-three exchange of nuptial cups with her bridegroom—her beloved *saru* monkey stuffed animal. "...My mother and grandmother."

After dessert, the group as a whole left, and she and Marcus walked next door to the house he was buying. Keiko truly appreciated being coddled by Marcus' sisters and sisters-in-law, so she wasn't expecting it when he said, "My brothers were talking after you ladies went in the kitchen, and... I think they're right, Keiko. I think we should consider at least telling your brother about our wedding. Someday you might regret not having anyone in your family at your wedding. In truth, what can your family do to stop our wedding? You're a grown woman. Maybe we should confront this now."

She swallowed in shock. His sisters' reactions had

convinced her she was doing the right thing by keeping the wedding quiet. How could his brothers have such an opposite reaction to the situation? "You don't know my parents, Marcus. They still consider it their place to make my decisions. I only went into medical missions and worked at the children's hospital in Nagasaki because they allowed it—that's the way they think. They would never consider that I made those decisions on my own. Until I'm married—married to the man they've chosen for me—and under his protection, they won't see any life decision as mine to make."

He looked slightly annoyed. "Protection? Don't you mean control?"

"In some ways, yes. Oh, Marcus, I thought we'd already talked about this. I haven't changed my mind. In fact, I'm surer than ever that telling them, even just telling Haruki, would be a mistake."

"Have you talked to him recently? Maybe he's come to his senses. Shouldn't we give him the opportunity?"

"I don't know, Marcus. But what's the harm in *waiting* for the inevitable confrontation? Why hurry the unpleasantness? We both know it'll come sooner or later. Besides, I'm used to my family not being around for the big events in my life: high school and college graduation, getting my medical degree… I promise you I won't regret not telling them."

At the steps of the front porch, he turned and put his arms around her. "I don't know, Keiko. It feels like we're hiding. Like we're doing something dishonest."

"But we're not. We're doing what we should. My parents are *not* part of our decision to spend our lives together. Nor is Haruki. This is my decision, *ours.* Isn't it, my love?"

He took a deep breath, nodding. "Yes. Of course. I just don't want... I don't want *anything* to happen to take you from me, Keiko. If there's some way we can prevent that..."

"You still think God's out to get you, don't you? That He doesn't want us to be together and will somehow prevent it? Because you left Japan, left missionary work?"

"My fears are superstitious," he conceded. "I know that, and I know I need to work through them. But I'm talking about something real here. If your parents come to the States to visit you and find out that we're married, that we didn't even bother to invite or tell them...they'll immediately distrust and dislike *me*."

Keiko shook her head. "I'll tell them that I wouldn't let you contact them. That I made the decision to keep them out of it."

He let out a noise of frustration. "That's not what I mean. How can they believe I'll take care of you, protect and put you above myself if I've already done the opposite? How can they respect me and trust that I'll do right by you?"

Keiko smiled teasingly. "You really are old-fashioned, aren't you, Marcus Samuels? Even by Western standards."

"And if I am?"

"I love you more," she assured him, wiggling up to him, hoping he would take her in his arms and kiss her.

He didn't disappoint. Best of all, he didn't bring up the subject of her family again that evening. Relieved, she found herself praying that contacting her family was now a closed issue.

Their marriage application bought and paid for, Marc felt as giddy as Keiko looked when they hugged outside the Administrative Center in La Crosse. "We're officially engaged," he murmured in wonder.

"It's like a dream come true. Nothing can go wrong now."

Even as Marc held the woman he loved close, he couldn't help wondering if she was right about that. He couldn't explain the urgency he'd been feeling lately. While he wouldn't push Keiko again on having her family attend their wedding, Haruki had been on his heart relentlessly of late. Believing that his long-time friend had chucked his Christianity in favor of illogical customs and rituals wasn't something Marc could truly get himself to believe Haruki had done. He was struggling, yes, but Marc believed that the Lord was trying to grow his friend in areas he'd let himself stagnate. *Just as He's been doing with me. I know He's not out to get me. Now I just have to get myself to believe it.*

After the last Bible study with his brothers and sisters, Keiko had said something that had gnawed on Marc for days afterward. She'd reminded him of what he'd told her about his arrival in Japan more than twelve years ago—that he'd joined WMMO because he believed the Lord was leading him there. Though he'd never been crazy about the idea of serving in another country, he'd given himself over to the directives in Romans 12:1-2. After that, Marc couldn't have anticipated what had happened to him once he arrived in Japan. Not simply the trauma he'd endured because of the panic attack that had come over him so suddenly on the plane, but also the fact that the Lord had never felt so far from him as during that time. Marc had been in the desert, and the sense of abandonment had been brutal.

For that first year of service, he'd questioned continuously whether he was truly doing any good. But he'd seen countless times that, even if God felt far away, His will was still being done through Marc. "Isn't that what you're going through now?" Keiko had said last Friday night. "Something tragic has happened. You lost your beloved mother, but deep down you know you're where God wants you to be and you're still following His will. Even in adversity, you continue to persevere. If that's not God's will, I don't know what is."

*Keiko's words made me remember that when I was little, my mom always somehow got me to see that God loves me and works through me in every circumstance, even if I'm torturously uncomfortable and miserable beyond consolation.*

He would continue to grieve the loss of his mother for the rest of his life, but he was feeling joy along with the devastation now—because of Keiko, their bright future, all their plans, and the daily embrace of his family. The house was almost ready, the loan just days away from being finalized. Marc had enjoyed the work involved in preparing the house so much, he'd been sleeping less than six hours a day, yet felt energized and renewed.

"Are you hungry?" he asked as they walked toward the parking lot, holding hands.

She nodded. "I'm starving."

"What are you in the mood for?"

"I think your sweet tooth is contagious. I feel like something decadent. Chocolate and ice cream and caramel and nuts..."

Marc chuckled. "You had me at chocolate, sweetheart."

Instead of a proper lunch, they shared an enormous banana split while discussing wedding plans. She'd already gotten her dress and everything that went with it—something fairy tale gorgeous but not 'wedding formal.' Marc had rented his tux ensemble. They'd booked the church and planned to decorate it themselves. Jay would perform the ceremony. His sisters had helped Keiko send out invitations, choose a cake and flower arrangements, plan the rehearsal dinner and reception down to napkins and music. Tamara's son Matt would be handling all the photography and videography. Marc's brothers were planning a bachelor party for him while the women were doing the same for Keiko. She'd said numerous times she didn't quite get the point of these since the only type of party she'd heard of before an American wedding included strippers and lots of alcohol—something neither of them found appealing in the least. Marc had explained that in his family, these 'clean' celebrations were more of a bon voyage to being single that involved little more than a sip of bubbly and a good meal.

In the meantime, Marc and Keiko were forced to endure a wedding prerequisite of premarital counseling on Wednesdays, just before the weekly church prayer meeting, something Marc hadn't been thrilled about at first but had soon realized Keiko needed. Because her parents hadn't modeled an ideal marriage for her, she knew little about things like realistic expectations, conflict resolution in a romantic relationship, intimacy and sexuality as well as making decisions for starting a family, and working together on long-term goals for their life together. They'd both found the sessions illuminating and helpful.

"The only thing left to get are the wedding bands," Keiko said.

They were sitting on the same side of the ice cream shop booth, and she looked up at him with eyes that suddenly made him feel hungry with need. When he kissed her, aware that he could easily lose control if he let himself, she blinked at him and gasped irregularly once he drew back from her. In a matter of weeks, she wouldn't be going across the street to his brother's house to sleep. They would share the same bed. They would have the kind of freedom he'd only dreamed of with the woman he'd committed his life and all-consuming loyalty to. Color flooded her glowing cheeks.

"What?" she murmured.

"There's one other thing I was hoping we could pick out today."

"Yes?"

"I want us to choose our marriage bed together." The full size bed he'd had in his apartment during college and med school would be adequate for their guest bedroom, but the bed they shared for the first time on their wedding night had to be special.

"You're planning our honeymoon night?" Keiko asked softly.

"Haven't you been?"

If possible, the high color in her face deepened. "Your sisters took me to a lingerie shop last Thursday, after lunch. I never believed there were so many possibilities..."

Realizing she was still shy about such things despite her openness whenever they shared intimacy that never crossed the line he'd drawn for them, Marc hugged her to him. All his life, he'd known his parents' love for each other crossed the possible planes— mental, spiritual, and most definitely physical. All his life, he and his siblings had seen them constantly kissing and touching, whispering to each other in private corners. Once Marc's brothers and sisters began to marry, he'd seen their parents' marriage mirrored in his siblings' and he'd begun to long for the intimacy marriage alone allowed. It'd never been his choice to be a bachelor—a virgin—for forty years. Soon that would be over, and he had every intention of enjoying a passionate sexual relationship with the woman he loved, starting on their wedding night. Keiko obviously felt the same, but he knew she wrestled with a sense of inadequacy and uncertainty in that department. He suspected once she saw and discovered for herself how desperately he wanted her and desired to show her how beautiful she was to him, how much he loved her, she would lose her justifiable inhibitions.

The next few hours only increased Marc's desire to be alone with his fiancée, but he also knew he needed to bring up the topic of talking to her brother again. The wedding was only days away. Together they gathered fresh leaves for their very hungry caterpillars in the aquarium, then brought them up to the largest bedroom in the house that would soon be theirs. The room was still empty, awaiting the matching furniture set they'd purchased earlier that day and that would arrive the following Monday.

While Keiko went about her daily task of caring for the insects that were currently sitting on a lone desk near the window—where they wouldn't wake him in the next room with their almost constant noisiness—Marc watched her, wondering how to bring up the topic of Haruki without putting her on the defense. "Have you talked to your brother lately?" he asked as casually as he could.

"He's called a few times. He left voice mails."

"Anything going on?"

"He just asked me to call him."

Whether he'd wanted to or not, he could feel her tensing before him. "Maybe...maybe he needs to talk to you, Keiko."

"What do you mean?"

Marc shook his head. "I can't explain it, but lately he's been on my mind almost constantly. I think we should call him. I think we should talk to him and tell him that we're planning to get married. He's your brother. He loves you, and once he's had a chance to really think about it, I know he wants the best for you. I think he's probably already realized that himself. Maybe he just wants to tell you."

"Or he wants to tell me something I don't want to hear. Didn't we agree to let this be, Marcus? I don't want to risk anything changing our plans."

"Why do you think anything will? Is there a possibility you'll change your mind about marrying me if your parents try to stop us?"

Her eyes wide with shock, she glanced back at him and then away quickly. "You don't know them. You don't understand what it's like to know...to know you have no choices. That your life has already been decided for you. *Not by you!* If I give them any chance at all, they'll try to stop this."

"So let them try."

She gasped as if she'd been punched in the stomach. "How can you say that?"

When she looked at him this time, her eyes were filled with unexpected tears. Shocking him with her abrupt reaction, she rushed out of the room and down the stairs. Marc only recovered from his paralysis with the slamming of the front door. Then he immediately started to follow her but realized maybe she needed time, needed to be by herself. He'd clearly said things she wasn't sure how to take. Given a little time alone to reflect, she might realize on her own that she needed to confront everything she'd been trying so hard to hide from.

His thoughts turned to prayer, but his cell phone rang and prevented him doing more than offering his heart, his longings, and his hopes for Keiko and their future up to the Lord. He recognized his father's new phone number on the screen and felt grateful that, between him and his father, they'd been keeping up daily calls. Without more than a few words of preface, Marc found himself telling his dad what had happened with Keiko a moment ago.

"You're afraid you're going to lose her," his father said, surprising him because, for the first time, Marc hadn't been thinking specifically about that aspect. How had his dad somehow gotten straight to the heart of the issue?

"I..." He sighed heavily. "I've got this picture in my head, Dad, of her parents showing up here. Objecting during our wedding ceremony, like you see on TV sitcoms all the time. And I admit, Keiko's fear about that happening makes me wonder if she'd go with them instead of marrying me."

Stephen's pause made Marc really consider the image he'd been pushing to the back of his mind. Did Keiko also fear she couldn't be strong enough to go through with their wedding?

"When I lost your mother, I was angry and I couldn't get myself to approach God with my fury. I avoided Him for weeks. You probably noticed I wasn't myself."

Marc couldn't say for sure his father was himself even now. Would he ever be again, without the woman he loved? *Will I be myself if Keiko doesn't go through with our marriage? I've planned out the rest of my life practically and the fact that she's worried about something going wrong, that she might not be able to go through with it...*

"The funny thing about fear is that it *grows* in the dark instead of shrinking. We can't contain it inside ourselves. The darkness feeds fear and it takes on a life of its own, bigger and more threatening to our well-being than we can imagine. Eventually, if we don't face our fear and bring it out into the light, it'll consume us."

*Dad's right. Why didn't I see the truth before? Is it possible to be afraid of fear? How ridiculous is that? And yet...*

"Son, it's okay to be honest. It was only when I was honest with the Lord about my anger that I started to let it go. Maybe the fact that you haven't done anything these past few weeks to upset the apple cart is why Keiko's fears have grown along with your own. Maybe you need to be honest and talk about them specifically. Maybe the two of you can work through them together."

Marcus was already starting down the stairs, realizing that he had a lot to learn about being in a romantic relationship himself. He'd barely scratched the surface in experiencing the ups and downs of love. One way or another, he and Keiko would work this out because he wasn't willing to let their fears consume them or tear them away from each other.

## Chapter 16

While rushing across the street, it became blindingly clear to Keiko that she'd reached a crossroad. If she didn't face this problem, she would abandon both her faith in Christ and her love for Marcus. She couldn't be a Christian in the world she'd come from, in which her duty to family and country would dictate that she marry an immoral man she didn't love and would eventually lose her identity and individuality to. The prospect of leaving Marcus... *Not loving him and being with him, not free to reach for him and touch him whenever I want and need is unbearable. The thought is almost as excruciating as the reality would be.*

As if her limbs had become too heavy to carry her on, she halted her flight and sat down on the curb in front of Justine and Joshua's home, as if she'd become a leaden being. Marcus had spoken the truth that was also inside her. For weeks, her brother had been calling and his messages had become increasingly insistent that she contact him. She'd relegated him to her voice mail because she couldn't get past the terror that filled her at possibly hearing him say it was too late—their parents were interceding on her behalf and would be here soon to talk sense into her. *They'll try to re-make me into the robot I was almost all my life until I came to the States and met free-spirited Jordan and her loving, Christ-led parents.*

Keiko had known she was wrong to avoid Haruki, just as she'd been wrong to get her back up whenever Marcus tried to broach the subject. *He's been following the will of God, the way he has all his life, and I've been fleeing it. But the bottom line comes to this now: I love the Lord, I love Marcus Samuels, and I'll do whatever I have to do to be with them. I have to be stronger than I've ever been before, stronger than I believe myself capable of being, to do this. But how?*

The front door of the home she and her new husband would soon share—if she hadn't messed up their chances at a life together—opened, and Marcus came out to the porch. His pleading gaze fixed on her. Even in the questionable light from the low-pressure, amber street lamps, she could see his love for her radiating from his entire being. In all honesty, she didn't know how she would find the strength to do what she knew she had to, but she couldn't deny her own heart. She jumped up and ran across the street, straight into his waiting arms.

"I'm sorry," they both said at once.

"No." She shook her head wildly. "You're absolutely right. I know you're right, and I've known it all the long. I just don't trust myself, even now."

"You think you'll cave in if your parents try to make you go home with them?"

"I would rather die."

He looked down at her in the porch glow. "What does that mean, sweetheart? Do you think you will or not?"

She couldn't say the words that filled her mind: *I'm betraying everything I am, everything I've ever known. My family! A Westerner can't understand the full scope of that. But Haruki does. And ultimately, we're both wrong for feeling that way if we let it ruin our faith and principles, our happiness, our very purpose.*

"We need to call Haruki. I know we do, Marcus. Let's do it now. Let's tell him we're getting married. Let's invite him to our wedding."

He obviously hadn't been expecting her abrupt capitulation. Goggling slightly at her, he demanded, "What about your parents?"

She clutched him tighter to her. "Marcus, please, be reasonable. I'm willing to admit all to Haruki, but let's invite my family...my parents and grandmother and sister...into our home *after* the honeymoon. We will tell them. I promise. But I still want to wait to tell them after our wedding. Can you do that and still respect me and yourself?"

Surprising her once more, he nodded. "I have to be honest with you, too, Keiko. I've lived in fear that your mother and father will show up on our wedding day and tell you to come home with them. And you'll go with them, leaving me standing there..."

Keiko cried out at the vivid image he'd painted with his words—an image that mirrored the one inside her darkest nightmares. Hating the idea that she'd caused him the same torment she'd put herself through, she nevertheless realized he was being honest with her instead of trying to protect her from his true fears. He'd been doing that all along. Now she owed him the same integrity. "That's my own fear, Marcus. That they'll come, and I'll feel the way I did all my life. I won't be able to deny the sense that I'm not free—I'm under their authority. I won't be strong enough to say, 'No. I have to do this my way. The Lord's way.' I'm sorry, Marcus. But I know, after our wedding, after our honeymoon, I'll have the strength I need. I'm sure of it. Please understand how new all this is for me. All I'm asking for is a little time to work this out the way that feels right to me." *The way that feels safe.*

"I admit, waiting to tell your parents until after we've been married for a few weeks feels right to me, too. I can't explain that, but let's pray about it, honey. Let's give this whole thing up to the Lord and let Him lead us. Let's be open to His leading instead of both acting like Jonah."

Even as they both chuckled, Keiko startled slightly at being called the unruly prophet. She suddenly saw herself in the analogy he'd made between himself and Jonah. She didn't like it any more than he had all this time.

They went back into the house and curled up together on the sofa, praying for aligned guidance and strength.

Then she called her brother. He answered within a few rings and she asked him if it was all right that she had him on speakerphone with her and Marcus. The cell phone was on the sofa between them. Her brother agreed with the arrangement.

"I'm sorry I've been avoiding you, Haruki," she started. "It's just..."

"You're married, aren't you? To Marcus-*san*?" he guessed. His tone wasn't accusatory or betrayed.

"No," Keiko insisted. "At least...not yet. I know you don't believe this, Haruki, but this is as much of a surprise for Marcus and me as it is for you. We didn't plan this. It just sort of happened."

"It's true, Haruki," Marcus added in a quiet voice.

"I suspect it's 'sort of been happening' for years, since the two of you met. You just didn't admit it to yourselves or each other until you didn't have anyone objecting to the possibility."

"Are you all right with this now?" Keiko asked carefully, feeling a bloom of hope in her chest based on her brother's tone of resignation.

"It wasn't easy, but yes, I've come to grips with it and seen the holes in my own Christianity because of it."

"Are you worried...well, that this will 'out' your faith to your family?" Marcus said with the gentleness Keiko knew her brother needed most of all right now.

"I guess that is what I've worried about more than I should have. I came to realize that I need this situation as much as Keiko probably does. Now I just have to get up the nerve..." he sighed, "...and get some leave from the hospital. But not now. Keiko's replacement has proven to need quite a bit of training. It's not a good time for me to leave, even for a short time."

Keiko helplessly worried that any delay would make him change his mind—she'd waffled the same way for so long. She still was, in areas, but couldn't imagine any other way to handle the impending confrontation.

"So...when is the ceremony?" Haruki asked.

Keiko gave him the date.

"You're sure there's no way you can join us?" Marcus asked with obvious disappointment.

"I wish I could. But I wish you both well. When are you planning to tell our family, Keiko?"

"In a month or so."

Haruki chuckled. "When the deed is done and there's no way back to virginal innocence? That's probably the wisest thing you can do, *imōto*. I know you and Marc will be happy together. He'll take care of you, Keiko."

"I will. I want you to know that, Haruki. Your sister is the most important person in my life. I only want to make her happy and keep her safe."

"I know you will, Marc-*san*. I'll never doubt."

"Thanks, Haruki."

Keiko had never expected to get her brother's

blessing and hadn't realized how much she needed it either. Fighting tears, they exchanged traditional farewells and well-wishing.

Once they hung up, she hugged Marcus. "Thank you for encouraging me to do that. My wedding day would have been tainted without Haruki's approval."

"For me, too."

The sense of rightness consumed her, replacing the fears and tension she'd been resisting for weeks. Unfortunately, she realized the evening was getting late. "Maybe I should go."

She rose, but Marcus took her hand and eased her back down on his lap. "Just a little longer," he murmured.

The untamed excitement she'd experienced so fiercely in their adjoined hotel rooms in Minnesota and then again countless times since expanded inside her until she could hardly breathe for anticipation. She knew Marcus would kiss her like that again now, and she reveled in their passion when he did. This was only a small taste of how it would be for them when they were married, when they could share their love with their bared bodies and souls. Marcus alone had made her realize the possibilities of such a union.

"Do you have any idea how much I want you, Keiko?" he asked in a harsh whisper, his hands cradled around her face.

"Some idea," she admitted. "I..." She couldn't help her blush or her instinct toward shyness.

"What, my love?"

"I can't wait."

Fiery love consumed his dark eyes and he kissed her again, so deeply, she could feel corresponding fires igniting in places that had been dormant all her life.

"Soon," Marcus promised.

Keiko closed her eyes in agony. The handful of days suddenly might as well be an eternity she wasn't sure how she'd get through.

Standing on the porch of his house, Marc was just about to dash across the street to Joshua's house for his bachelor party when his cell phone rang. He pulled it out to see Haruki's phone number on the screen. Pushing the receive button, he brought the phone to his ear. "Haruki?"

"Is Keiko with you?" his friend asked.

"No. She's having her bachelorette party. I was just heading to my bachelor bash."

"Maybe it's for the best," Haruki murmured.

Confused, Marc laughed. "That we're having parties the night before the wedding? Or that Keiko isn't with me?" He glanced across the street. It was raining buckets. Family members had been darting through it to Josh's house or to Jay and Ashley's for Keiko's party. The rehearsal dinner had actually been a rehearsal *lunch* so the parties could take place this evening.

"Listen, Marc-*san*, I've been thinking a lot about the last time we talked. About my witness to my family. I realize now that my faith may be the only way my wife and children, my parents, grandmother and younger sister ever hear about the Lord."

"Unfortunately true," Marc agreed.

"The realizing catapulted me. I don't know how else to describe the feeling inside me. I took emergency leave, I went home, and I talked to my wife about my faith...and my desire for a passionate relationship with her."

Marc tried to hide his shock in the enthusiastic encouragement he offered: "That sounds like a step in the right direction, Haruki. I'm proud of you."

"I thought it was a step in the right direction at first, too. But Gin—what was that word you used to use?—freaked out? She didn't want anything to do with my inappropriate attentions or my Christian God."

It was unimaginable to Marc that a wife could be so against the idea of a continuous passionate relationship with the man she'd chosen, whether personally or out of a sense of duty, to spend her life with, to have children with. "I'm sorry, my friend," Marc said sincerely.

"Unfortunately, she wasn't content to leave it at that. Gin told my parents and grandmother everything—how I've become a Christian and abandoned Japanese ways. Needless to say, my parents aren't happy. They feel I've betrayed them—our family and our country. They assumed Keiko's done the same, given her unwillingness to stay in touch all this time and her time being Westernized. They know about you, Marc-*san*. They know she's going to abandon her *omiai* marriage promise to Ryu. Yumako must have been talking to them about the changes in Keiko and me before this, and they made a whole series of connections. My father, especially, is so upset, he's claiming Keiko has been brainwashed by all the Americans she knows. He believes it's his place to retrieve her, bring her home and talk Japanese sense back into her."

Marc swallowed, recognizing the fear he and Keiko had worried about coming to fruition. "You think he'll come here?"

Haruki didn't pause, but spoke in a firm, quiet voice. "Yes."

"When?"

"I have no idea. I told him I would give him your address, but not until after your wedding. If he wants to find Keiko sooner, he'll have to go about it in another way. I felt you needed to know, Marc-*san*. You might want to wait until after the wedding to tell Keiko any of this."

Marc knew as well as her brother did that Keiko would be upset by this—upset to the point that she might not go through with the wedding. She wouldn't be able to relax before, during or after... *If she's told.*

"I'm sorry the confrontation didn't go better, Haruki," Marc said. If his friend was anything like him, he would take his family's reaction the wrong way— he would assume he'd gone against the Lord's will because his witness has been rejected so thoroughly, forgetting that Christ hadn't promised success each time a Christian went out into the world and gave the Good News to souls in need of His salvation.

"I couldn't have turned back from talking to my wife, Marc-*san*. Maybe this had to happen. Maybe it has to happen to you and Keiko. I'm sorry, though, if anything stands in the way of your marriage."

The burden on Marc's mind followed him through nearly every moment of the bachelor party, and he seriously considered not telling Keiko—not telling her until he had no other choice. *In other words, when her father shows up.* But some sane part of Marc accepted that he couldn't enter into a marriage he wanted to last for a lifetime by keeping secrets from the woman he loved.

When the party next door broke up and cars began to drive away, he dashed through the rain to the parish without an umbrella. Keiko was helping to clean up and Marc pitched in cheerfully, despite her frequent comments that he was soaked and should dry off. He hoped that he could have time alone with her sooner if they got the work done. Ashley teased them about not seeing each other before the wedding and ended up having to explain the American tradition, or superstition, to Keiko.

The rain hadn't let up at all when Marc asked for a few minutes to talk to her in private before he walked her to Josh and Justine's. They made it to his house under the big umbrella Ashley insisted they take. Inside, he kicked off his shoes and went to get a towel. She found him with his shirt and socks stripped off in the bathroom upstairs toweling his dripping hair. "What's going on?" she asked, her tone an indication that she was expecting something.

Knowing he couldn't soften this blow, he told her all about Haruki's call without preface. She listened without saying a word, but he saw the grief claiming her expression. She'd dreaded exactly this.

"Do you think your father will come here?" Marc asked her, tossing the wet towel over the shower rod.

"Yes," she said without hesitation. "But I'm not sure when."

"So...what do you want to do?" he asked, moving to her side. She immediately put her face and warm hands against his cold chest. Marc's pulse jumped and he tried to control himself enough to offer her the support she would need to get through this. "Would it help to call your parents and make your stand on the issues clear?"

She sighed, her fingers caressing his chest and making him nearly insane with her inadvertently erotic caresses. He finally had to take both of her hands in his and draw them away from his too-eager body.

"Marcus, I asked you to trust me before, and I'm asking you again. I can't call my parents. I've made my choice, and there's nothing they can do to change my mind. But I know if I phone them tonight, they'll see the act as a request on my part. They'll believe I'm asking them for permission to undertake this path. I can't give them that kind of control. I told you we would call them and tell them together, and we will— in a month. If they come here instead, we'll tell them when their appearance becomes a reality. Otherwise...tomorrow is going to be the most perfect, happy day of my life. I won't allow anything to ruin it."

"What do you want me to do, Keiko?" he asked with a bit of uncertainty.

"Stand with me."

"I'll do that without question." And, if it came down to it, he would protect her if she needed him to. He didn't like having to wait for her to ask him for that protection, but he sensed in this situation that his father's advice was best. He had to give Keiko the opportunity to stand up for herself and her faith. If and when she needed his help, she would ask for it.

## Chapter 17

At her bachelorette party, Keiko had heard the
Victorian era wedding tradition of something old,
something new, something borrowed, something blue,
and a silver sixpence in her shoe. The morning of the
wedding, each of Marcus' sisters and sisters-in-law
presented her with one item of good luck within that
tradition. Then, for the two hours before the
ceremony, they helped her primp and preen. Her
spaghetti strap, column dress with a high-low hemline
was made of chiffon and adorned with floral hand-
sewn silver and clear glass beading.

She'd never felt more beautiful in her life as when
her eyes met Marcus' during her walk down the aisle.
The love and adoration in his eyes made her feel
invincible. Whatever happened, she refused to allow
her family to separate her from the life-altering love
she'd found. He slipped her arm through his and held
her close to him once they turned to his brother at the
front of the family church.

She couldn't help comparing the ceremony to the
ones she'd been to in the past. Japanese weddings
were drastically different. Even Jordan's 'event of the
century' wedding had been radically dissimilar. But
Keiko's wedding was everything she wanted, all she'd
dreamed it would be.

She felt the love and joy emanating from Marcus'
family and she anticipated the rest of her life in the
words she exchanged with her beloved groom: "I love
you and thank the Lord for the love that has bound our
hearts and lives together as one in the spiritual
fellowship of marriage. I promise to love, honor, and

cherish you always. As we enter into the privileges and joys of a pure relationship blessed by God, I look forward to being together on the great adventure of building a Christian home. I promise to always look to Christ as Head of our home. I promise to love you in sickness as in health, in poverty as in wealth, in sorrow as in joy, and I bind myself to you and you alone by God's grace, trusting in Him, so long as we both live."

When they kissed and sealed their vows before God and so many of their loved ones, she had tears in her eyes. Nothing could stop them now. She intended to enjoy every minute that followed this one—the reception and their first night together as husband and wife—and not worry about a single thing.

"Don't be nervous," Marc said softly when Keiko came out of the bathroom wearing an elegant, sexy nightgown that showed tantalizing glimpses of satiny skin and warm, flushed flesh. He could hardly wait to touch and be touch, to share the ultimate intimacy. He'd worried she'd take a long time getting ready, but she'd come out in mere minutes. Instantly, seeing her, he'd been ready.

"I'm not nervous," she murmured, moving into his arms. "Nothing can go wrong now."

Marc understood exactly what she meant. Both of them had expected an angry father to burst into the church or the reception, demanding a halt to the blasphemous proceedings, before he tried to drag her off to the family home she'd grown up in—the one that would become her prison, if she allowed it. Instead, from start to finish, their day had been perfect. Even the rain that had been plaguing them for weeks on end had stayed away. They'd had blue skies and sunshine. The only thing left was satisfying each other, in every way.

From the first, deep kiss, Marc knew their union would be perfect and it was. Keiko gave herself with the same abandon he gave her, and they found blissful freedom in learning to pleasure each other. They both had tears in their eyes when they came back from heaven, and he rolled them to their sides, still holding her body close to his. "Worth the wait?"

"Oh, yes," she agreed breathlessly.

"For me, too. How could anyone ever lose this passion? Let go of it? I'll never..."

"Promise me, Marcus."

"I promise. We'll be like this for the rest of our lives. I'll always want you, I'll want you more and more. You're so beautiful. You know what you do to me. This is an easy promise. I love you more than anything."

She was smiling and crying when she kissed him with infinite tenderness. "Do you think we've made a baby, my love?"

The idea energized him. To have a child with this woman... How much more happiness could he stand? "If not now," he murmured, dipping his head to kiss her again with very definite intentions, "then soon."

"Hmm."

Hours later, they crept downstairs to raid the refrigerator. "Isn't the floor cold?" she said, looking at his bare feet on the hardwood floor. She wore her functional black slippers.

"Not to me. I plan to never wear slippers again. Whether or not the floor is cold."

Keiko giggled effusively.

All the years he'd been a medical missionary in a strange country, he'd somehow found it simplicity itself to slip back into habits he hadn't practiced except on his infrequent vacations home. The hard part had been forcing himself to become a person he wasn't and could never be, following rules and regulations that made no sense to him. Here, even Keiko had abandoned many of the traditions she'd lived by in Japan because they'd been expected of her there. Maybe for the first time, she could be who she was and not feel she was doing something wrong for it.

On a satisfied exhale, Marc put his arms around her at the table where they'd settled to nibble on their snack. "I love you, Keiko, whether you wear slippers or run around barefoot. I'll accept you even if you someday go against proper etiquette and put sugar in your tea. I never want you to be anyone but who you are."

"That's made all the difference in the world, Marcus. I think that's why I could never be without you. Always, you've loved me for me."

"And you've loved me."

She hugged him close almost desperately. "We're married. We're together. We can share everything. We'll be together forever. Nothing could possibly go wrong now."

Marc didn't want to consider the one thing that *could* taint their joy. But he knew for a fact that he and Keiko would have to face what was standing in the way of their total happiness. Sooner or later, she would have to come out of hiding and face the greatest hardship she'd probably ever have to.

## Chapter 18

Eight days later, Keiko discovered for herself the meaning of the words "blushing bride." She hadn't been around people for a gloriously secluded week—hadn't been outside in that time, other than the private gardening she and Marcus had been doing in their new backyard. They'd tilled and prepared the soil, planted and fertilized and watered vegetable and butterfly gardens. She hadn't realized how hard it would be to give time and devotion to anyone else after so many tasks that included only her and Marcus. A week didn't seem like enough time to become so immersed in their own little world, but she realized Sunday morning just how much she'd coveted the time alone with her new husband.

After church, they attended the family potluck, but they barely left each other's side during that time. Their eyes met and held meaningfully the few times they'd been separated by various family members.

Just after lunch, when they were trying hard to slip unobtrusively away, one of his brothers teasingly asked if the two of them were planning to hole up in their house forever. Marcus put his arm around her, drawing her back to him on the outdoor chaise lounge chair they shared. He smiled at her lovingly...then completely turned the subject away from their obsession for each other. "We've been talking about opening a peds clinic in Peaceful. Soon. But not too soon."

"Both of you?"

Keiko nodded. "Until we can start our family. I'll stay home with the children until they're old enough to go to school."

One of Marcus' many young nieces approached them. "Keiko, there's a man at the front of the house asking for you. He doesn't seem to speak English."

In shock, Keiko looked from the messenger to Marcus and back to the girl. "Doesn't speak English?"

"I think maybe he's your father."

Both she and Marcus rose as one. She didn't feel coordinated at all and was grateful when he gripped her arm to steady her. "Marcus," she murmured, as if she was bleeding her fear.

"We knew it would happen," he said quietly with his mouth against her ear. "I'd just hoped we'd have more time."

*More time? For what? I've never in my life stood up to my father. I never believed I should, would, or might have to.* She flushed, abruptly aware that she was shaking with a violence she couldn't have anticipated. Marcus must have felt it, too. They'd made their way halfway around to the front of the parish when he stopped her abruptly and pulled her into his arms. "It'll be all right, Keiko. I promise. I won't leave your side...unless you ask me to."

"Don't. Don't leave," she begged, holding on to him tight enough to inflict bruises. He didn't protest.

"Okay."

She didn't get a chance to be assured of her bearings. Some part of her that she couldn't fathom was taking this development as a loss—as the potential for forfeiting everything that mattered to her. Her father rounded the corner, and though she recognized him on sight, she acknowledged how long it'd been since she'd seen him. He looked considerably older than the last time she'd gone home.

With what little strength she possessed, she

reluctantly eased out of Marcus' arms and greeted her father with a deep, honorific bow. Marcus did the same. Her father nodded at her, but he stepped forward and shook Marcus' hand. Keiko understood without a word that her father was treating him like an outsider with the foreign gesture. Both men spoke formal greetings, but her father refused to speak American even after the courtesies were exchanged. Being loyal to their culture by highlighting her lack of similar duty was obvious in the unspoken scorn in his demeanor. His coldness increased when Marcus spoke fluent Japanese, insisting that he be introduced to his family properly. In all ways, Keiko felt proud of how her husband created an environment of respectful openness and welcome that would have shamed her father if Marcus had intentionally or inadvertently reacted with ill breeding.

Keiko couldn't help noticing how different her father was from everyone else present, even Marcus' father, who was his age. Her father was as small as she herself was but rotund, his ebony hair streaked with silver and slicked back with styling wax. His face was pinched yet flat, white, with an abundant sprinkling of liver spots and small, furtive eyes. *Do I also look so different to everyone here?* she wondered uncomfortably. She hadn't felt 'foreign' for so many years—since high school with Jordan, where she and Haruki had stood out so distinctly from the other kids. Jordan had called them exotically beautiful then, but it'd taken Keiko a long time to actually feel she wasn't an alien.

Once the greetings were completed, Marcus suggested the three of them go next door and "get caught up." Keiko's father agreed, and after three refusals, at last allowed Marcus to take his suitcase that he'd carried all the while. As they walked toward the house, Keiko noticed no new cars—rental or otherwise—parked along the familiar street. Her father must have taken a taxi—from the La Crosse Municipal Airport? Or the international airports in Madison or Milwaukee? She wasn't sure he understood American currency. How much had he unwittingly paid?

She asked, "How are *Okaa-san* and *Obaa-san*? Did they come with you?"

He shook his head but said nothing until they arrived next door. Marcus offered tea and her father accepted. Keiko insisted on preparing it, her ears alerted when her father asked what was happening, what had happened here. Marcus could have so easily played dumb, but he responded without hesitation or uncertainty, "Keiko and I were married last weekend, Oichi-*sama*."

The time that followed was the most uncomfortable Keiko had ever endured. Her father let loose his fury at her betrayal—on both of them. With as much patience as calmness, Marcus spoke to him without any sign of defensiveness, still using honorific respect in his word choices. Over and over, her father said, "You're not one of us. You can't understand our ways."

Unable to speak, Keiko realized that she felt ashamed and she hated the feeling because she wasn't entirely sure *what* she was ashamed of. She only knew that she'd disappointed her father deeply and she couldn't deny that the realization devastated her. *I might as well be a little girl again, as I was the day my father formally asked me if I would marry Ryu during the* omiai. *"Of course, Father. Whatever you think is best." He expected me to agree with whatever he, my mother and my grandmother suggested...and he still does. I've never defied him. The thought would have been unimaginable. It remains so, even now. The "grown-woman" argument seems to mean nothing although I'm thirty-three years old and married.*

In part, she realized that this confrontation had to be between her father and her new husband, and Marcus represented himself extremely well. Even she could see that when her father paused and began asking Marcus questions about his medical education and work, the sacrifices he'd made in the missionary field, and even about his Christianity that he was impressed. Marcus spoke with a confidence and assurance that couldn't be denied and was even captivating in its own way. Oh, how she wished she could steal a small bit of that innate ability. But when persecution arose, she fled and went into hiding, or worse, she crumpled and folded. It was her normal state of being. She didn't know how to stand up for herself. Never before had she tried.

When she became aware that the light was fading in the kitchen, she glanced at the clock to see that hours had passed. Marcus and her father were still fully engaged in their conversation. Her father remained mildly rigid, yet he'd reluctantly begun conversing in English. Keiko wondered if he'd even noticed he was doing so.

Unobtrusively, she got up and began preparing a traditional Japanese meal, pitiful appeasement, but the ritualistic tasks were a relief to her. When she served them the evening meal at the oversized black oak coffee table in the living room—the closest they had to the *Chabudai* table Keiko had grown up with in their *tatami* room—both men ate without complaint while continuing their conversation about "the Christian God and this strange religion." Keiko ate little, unsurprised that her father was so intrigued. He'd always been all over the place in his spirituality. Even his own family members found him odd and superstitious. Had Haruki tried to talk to him about any of this? Even if he had, Keiko couldn't imagine her father accepting the authenticity of Christianity from his children, in word or deed. He only listened now so raptly because he considered Marcus an outsider.

"*Otō-san*, we have room here in our home. Please spend the night," Keiko invited after she'd cleaned up their meal.

He shook his head. "I have booked a return flight for the two of us, *musume*."

"It's already late, *Otō-san*."

For a long moment, he looked at her. Then he simply, yet unfathomably, nodded. Keiko rose and went to make up the guest bedroom. *He's booked a return flight for both of us. He still believes I'll go with him because he expects me to. I can't leave Marcus...but how can I stand up to my father and defy him any further than I already have?*

In the Japanese culture women deferred to men, and Keiko did that in a way Marc had never quite seen her do before. *I underestimated her fear of going up against her father. She warned me about that, and she'd been right that I didn't really know or understand her parents. I didn't realize the full scope of their relationship—I don't know my own wife in this regard.*

She went to bed first, after showing her father his room and explaining the bathroom accommodations—

so different from his native country.

"That didn't go so badly," Marc said with more cheerfulness than he felt once he closed the door of their bedroom. "He actually listened to our Christian witness. He was interested."

"*Your* Christian witness. I said and did nothing. I told you my father is extremely superstitious and open to 'spiritual diversions.'"

Marc had noticed everything she'd said—and *hadn't* said. During the hours with her father visiting, she'd gone utterly quiet and pliant in a strange way he'd had little experience seeing her adopt, and her father had been almost animatedly interested in the ways of the "Christian God." He shrugged at her response. "All in all, I think it went well."

Keiko gaped at him. "You don't honestly believe he's accepting all of this? That he'll willingly leave without me tomorrow? You and I have only been married a week, Marcus. He'll try to get me to annul our marriage."

*And now it comes down to it.* Marc shoved his hands in the pockets of his dress trousers. "What happens from here on out is your choice, Keiko. He'll only leave here with you if *you* let him. He can't legally annul our marriage unless *you* want that to happen. America is a free country, and he has no rights over you here, if he even does in your home country. Will you allow him to have control of this situation?"

She shook her head, closing the distance between them quickly. "You know I don't want to do any of those things," she said, putting her arms around him and obviously willing him to take her in. He did because he couldn't leave her out in the cold. "Oh, Marcus. You can't understand."

"I think I heard that enough tonight to last me a

lifetime."

She sighed. "There's an old Japanese saying: There are four things in life to be feared. Earthquakes, thunder, fire...and fathers."

"He didn't seem all that intimidating to me, Keiko. Just the opposite. I know in your culture, you're instilled with a deathly fear of disobedience, of being strong and independent. But I don't think you're seeing the situation clearly, honey."

"What do you mean?"

"I mean, your view of *yourself* is all wrong. You're not like a hand fan that folds with the slightest pressure. Remember while we were picking leaves for the Luna moth caterpillars yesterday, you were telling me about woolly bear caterpillars? How they tend to blend into their environment?"

"And curl into a tight ball when threatened," she murmured in self-defeat.

"And didn't you tell me that same caterpillar transforms into a brilliant Tiger Moth? Teddy bear transformed into tiger. They can be poisonous and the larval 'hairs' can sting. If a threat is perceived, that moth really shows its colors."

"You think I'm capable of that, Marcus? Do you know me at all?"

The defeat in her tone made him almost insane with the ease she was letting herself surrender. "What if you're pregnant?" he asked quietly, his tone hard. "There's been ample opportunity for it to happen in the last week."

She looked up at him with an expression that could only be described as uncertain fear. Up until that point, she'd been eagerly sharing his hope of becoming pregnant. She closed her eyes.

"I love you, Keiko. That's the truth. You're my

entire life. I want to spend the rest of my days with you. But I can't make this decision for you, honey."

She hugged him hard, pressing her face against his chest as if she felt helpless and lost. Marc remembered his father's words about this: *"Then all of these things will have to be faced and dealt with, each in its turn. All you can do is be there for her and love her. Stand with her when the storm comes. But, at the time when she needs you to, son, you'll have to let her go by trusting and believing in her. Ultimately, what she does is her choice and it's her battle to fight. If she comes back to you when it's over, you'll have her for all eternity."*

He remembered, knew what had to do...and he prayed.

## Chapter 19

Keiko didn't understand herself. She knew she could never give up Marcus and the perfect life they'd only just begun to build together. Yet, after an inconsequential protest against making love with her father so near, she conceded that this decision wasn't as easy as it should have been. Much as she wished she could casually shrug off the loss of her family, she wasn't that type of person. Maybe some would consider most of her life the result of a brainwashing technique that prevented her from going against the duties, traditions and loyalties of her family and her country. The fact was, she felt strong ties to every part of her early life just as strong as the ties she'd made since coming to the United States and giving her life to Christ.

Surprising herself, she woke at eight a.m. and realized she must have crashed sometime following her last look at the clock around three in the morning. The bed beside her was empty, and she turned her body toward the place that had become Marcus'. She saw a scrap of paper lying on his pillow and dragged it forward to read his spidery handwriting.

*I called the realtor, and I'm going to get the layout of some office space in town. I'll be back later. Enjoy your time with your father. All my love, M.*

Keiko closed her eyes and hugged the note to her chest. She knew exactly what her husband was doing, and she wasn't sure whether to be glad or upset. He believed whatever she decided to do about her father's expectation that she would return home with him after annulling their marriage was her decision. She knew what he wanted. He was leaving her to do whatever she wanted. His actions couldn't have been natural or comfortable for him. Marcus was a natural protector. She didn't doubt for a second that his first instinct had been to tell her father to get on the plane and not to look back—that she belonged to him and letting some immoral heathen have her in some insane betrothal would be over his dead body. A part of her wished he'd let his natural instincts take over, that he'd make the decision for her so she wouldn't have to make it for herself. *But I know he loves me too much to hold onto me if it's not what I really want. And he wants to know that I'm with him by choice, not force. How can I do anything but love him more for loving me enough to let me go if that's what I want? But I love him too much to leave him. I know I have to stand up for myself with my father. I have to stand up for my faith and my love and my own life and choices.*

From downstairs, she heard the sound of rattling and started to a sitting up position. Her father was awake, fending for himself in the kitchen. Keiko jumped out of bed and dressed quickly, wishing she had time to arrange herself properly.

She found her father making tea in the kitchen. "Let me get this, *Otō-san*."

Agreeably, he went to sit at the kitchen table while she prepared tea, served him, then made *asa-gohan*, miso soup, grilled fish, and pickles for their breakfast. Just as they had for the evening meal last night, they ate seated on the living room floor before the coffee table. The conversation was stiff and formal, and she was surprised he allowed her to update him on what she'd been doing in the last few years since she'd last seen him and the rest of her family. He also informed her of the activities and health of each person in their *ikka*, household. It was at the end of the meal, while they lingered over the green tea, that he said in stubborn Japanese, "But you will be home soon. You will be with us once more."

A strange compulsion washed over Keiko. Forcefully, she began detailing her future to her father. "Marcus is meeting with a realtor today to look at office space. We're planning to open a pediatric clinic in Peaceful. We'll both work as doctors in our clinic until I get pregnant. Like Mother, I plan to devote myself to our children. They'll be so important in our lives..."

*"Shitsuke?"*

Discipline of children in Japan could be simplified into the statement of being the type of upbringing where cleanliness, neatness, keeping things in order was of utmost importance. But at its core, *shitsuke* was about conforming and doing what had been decided— by Japanese customs, traditions and duties to family and country. Keiko knew she couldn't be drawn into that discussion with her father—because raising their children would be the responsibility of her and Marcus alone. "Marcus isn't so different than you in that regard, *Otō-san*. Family is the core of his life. I love him passionately. I can't imagine that ever changing. Even before I realized that he was my life, I aligned my life—everything I am and want to be—with his desires and dreams. I came to the States with him whenever he scheduled a vacation. I've been a citizen here since I turned eighteen. I still have my apartment in Chicago, but soon Marcus and I will go and get my things so we can be here together, with nothing holding us back." For a long minute following her speech, she stared across the table at her father, waiting for him to speak and try to dispute her decisions.

"You are not thinking clearly, *musume*. That has been clear to me since I arrived. Once you are away from this influence, surrounded once more by your mother and grandmother and sister and sister-in-law, you will see things as they really are. You have already made your marriage promise to another. You cannot lay aside one for another so easily. Your mother did not raise you in that manner."

"I love Marcus. He's everything to me. I've never loved Ryu. I never will. I don't respect him, and I could never bind myself to a man like him. And I belong to the Christian God that Marcus is committed to. Nothing will ever change my commitments to Marcus and the Christian Lord. But I love my family, *Otō-san*. Even if I can't be who and what you expect me to be, I love you."

Her father's expression was determined, and she understood that he wouldn't allow himself to be influenced by her words. "Once you are back where you belong, you will get away from the silly captivation you have for this round-eye. I can see that he seduced you, Keiko...possibly before the ceremony he arranged to bind you to him. This can be corrected easily with an annulment. You will see that tradition and duty are your truest honor, my daughter. We will leave as soon as you have packed. Until you are ready, I will stroll the gardens I saw from my room window upstairs."

He rose and left the house through the back French doors. For a long minute, Keiko sat, frustrated. Then she rose and cleaned up the meal. She went to shower, telling herself she would never live up to her father's expectations. After she'd prepared for the day properly, she called Marcus' cell phone. "Where are you?"

"We were just about to look at some of these buildings."

"Can you wait for me? I can be there in ten minutes."

"Of course."

He didn't say anything else, though she knew he wanted to. Disconnecting, she went outside and announced to her father that she was going into town. Would he like to accompany her? He said nothing, just looked at her as if her stubbornness was vexing him. When he continued his silence, she closed the French doors behind her and walked through the house to the front door. She had no idea what her father planned to do at this point. Would he leave the country without saying goodbye to her? Would she ever speak to or see her family again if he did? The idea was devastating to her, but, when she saw Marcus' face—the tension there—she knew she'd done the right thing.

He hugged her hard enough to leave bruises. "How are things?"

She shrugged. "I don't know at this point. I have no idea what my father's going to do. But I know I'm staying exactly where I belong. With my beloved, sexy husband."

Despite the realtor approaching, Marcus kissed her passionately, and Keiko couldn't feel anything but elated.

Keiko's appearance and reassurance carried Marc blissfully through the promising tours of several spacious office buildings and a shopping trip to restock their kitchen. But his tension started once more when they returned home and carried in the dozen grocery bags to find her father still there. Nothing was spoken about his plans, whether he continued to expect Keiko to leave here with him. In fact, the man was bursting with questions—about the medical practice they planned to open soon, as well as their "Christian God."

The weather was gorgeous, the sun brilliant and warm. The entire world seemed alive with birds singing and colorful insects fluttering past the open windows. While they talked well into the afternoon and early evening, Marc suggested they go out to the back garden, where he grilled up thick, juicy steaks. They ate crunchy-tender, buttery asparagus, creamy potato salad—Marc's mother's recipe—and strawberry shortcake, and her father ate heartily. Marc knew Keiko was surprised about that because she'd expected him to cling to Japanese ideals here, down to his eating habits. He even offered a traditional reception of gratitude following the meal. The man was relaxed tonight in a way Marc began to suspect Keiko had never seen before.

"I can't help wondering if God is keeping him here," Marc said later while he and Keiko prepared for bed in their room.

"I don't mean to be disbelieving, Marcus, but if he did come to faith in Christ, he would simply mesh it into his other Japanese beliefs and superstitions."

"We don't know what God is planning."

"No. I suppose we don't."

Her tone was pessimistic, and Marc pulled her into his arms, tossing the nightgown she held in her hand off to a nearby chair.

"Marcus..." she began her protest, just as she had the night before.

"What?" He kissed his way down her glorious throat.

"My father..."

"...didn't hear a thing last night and he won't tonight either. I promise." He smiled seductively, and she melted against him when he added, "Let's make love, sweetheart."

She gave in easily, unable to resist their passionate desire for one another any more than he could. He couldn't deny that something about the situation they were facing seemed to make her more aggressive and equally vulnerable than ever before. Both of them were shaking violently once the tumult passed and they clung to each other, panting, in the aftermath.

"You're so perfect for me, Keiko. I love everything about you. I'll never get enough of you."

She snuggled closer to him. "I feel the same, Marcus. We're so blessed."

They prayed together, and he couldn't help kissing her again, aware that his satiation only moments before had been temporary. Unfortunately, a cell phone rang and Keiko rushed to answer it so her father wouldn't be woken. Marc knew she was embarrassed about their current activity, explaining why she handed the call off to him instantly after she pressed the talk button.

"My father's there, isn't he?" Haruki greeted Marc with.

"I assumed you gave him our address," Marc said. He glanced at Keiko, covering them both with the blanket as if her brother could see them. Marc grinned.

"No. He got it some other way. So he is there?"

"Since Sunday."

"How's it going?"

"A little tense but mostly good. He's insisting your

sister return home with him, but he's also been extremely open to hearing about faith in Christ."

"You're not surprised about that, are you, Marc-*san*?"

"I shouldn't be, according to Keiko."

"I haven't been any kind of witness to my family. Only recently did I stand up for my faith."

"You'll get many chances to be a witness, I promise you, Haruki. Don't beat yourself up. God may have been holding you from it until now, until such a time as this. Your father *is* receptive to 'the Christian God.' That may also mean the rest of your family could come to the same place in the future."

Surprising him, Haruki wasn't pessimistic about how that outcome would be, as Keiko had been. He said he would be praying for them during this time and to keep him updated. Marc assured him he would.

"Haruki?" Keiko guessed when he hung up and set the phone aside. "He guessed our father was here?"

"Yes. I appeased his worry." Marc slid fully beneath the covers with her. "Now, where were we?"

## Chapter 20

Keiko sat bolt upright in the bed after what could have only been a half hour of sleep. What had woken her in such a shocking manner instantly became clear. Someone was screaming. Marcus had already leapt from the bed and was yanking on pants.

"What..."

"Your dad," he told her.

Keiko threw back the covers, pulling on her robe while shoving her feet into her slippers, then followed Marcus at a dead run down the hall to her father's room. Marcus knocked briefly, opened the door and turned on the overhead light in the guest bedroom.

When he glanced at Keiko expectantly, she rushed to her father's side. She saw that he'd arranged a bed for himself on the floor out of the linen and blanket. His screams had subsided, but he was sitting up on his makeshift bedroll, breathing harshly, his head in his hands. "What is it, *Otō-san*? Are you all right?"

"A vision," he told them, gasping. "I have had a vision. An omen." He looked up, his gaze stealing fearfully to Marcus. "From your Christian God. He admonished me that what He has joined together, man must not put asunder."

Keiko wondered if she or Marcus had mentioned that Bible verse at all during their conversations with her father. She couldn't recall that they had. Perhaps he'd heard it somewhere else. When she asked him more about the dream, he shook his head, insisting that he was fine and only wanted to go back to sleep.

Feeling lost and uncertain as to what had happened, she and Marcus returned to their bedroom and got back into their comfortable bed.

"You said he's had visions before?" Marcus said once he put his arms around her and urged her to lay her head on his chest.

"He calls them that. I'm not really sure how this is different from a nightmare."

"Could he have really had a visitation from God, warning him to back off?"

Keiko had never placed much stock in the visions she'd heard others talk about, especially her father's. He'd been superstitious all her life, following whatever had grabbed hold of him or terrified him at that time. She didn't expect that this vision would be any more than that, but she couldn't have predicted that she'd find him up first the next morning, his suitcase packed and waiting near the front door. He'd been reading, she realized, seeing a Japanese Bible in the browser of the laptop in the living room. *He was quietly reading while Marcus and I slept in and then showered together in the master bedroom.*

"I can make breakfast and then we can take you to the airport, *Otō-san*," Keiko began insistently.

He shook his head. "On the contrary, I am refreshed. I must return to our home. My flight is already scheduled, and I must go now."

She waited, glancing at Marcus, wondering if her father would press the issue of her returning with him. But he said nothing.

"Let us drive you to the airport," Marcus said three more times, even adding the customary, "It's nothing. No trouble at all." Her father also followed custom in modestly refusing the offer repeatedly before finally nodding agreeably.

The trip was beyond uncomfortable. Keiko didn't want to broach the subject of her accompanying her father. She knew Marcus certainly didn't. And her father seemed oddly content with the silence. He insisted again once they arrived at the airport that he didn't have time for breakfast, wasn't even hungry. His flight was leaving soon. Discomfort filled Keiko. Was this goodbye forever? Would her father leave, leave *her* willingly here with her chosen husband, and never explain his change of heart?

When he took his suitcase from Marcus inside the terminal, her father said in halting English, "I am not clear what happened to me last night. But I admit that I have never trembled in the presence of a god before. Last night, I believe I met a god for the first time, a true One. I do not know what it means, but something inside me is changed. I cannot explain this or what it means, but I am not the same man I was before I had that vision."

Her father's words were strange—and not simply because he didn't speak fluent English. Neither Keiko or Marcus knew what to say. There was no time to search for the proper words either. Her father's flight was called, and they exchanged traditional bows. Surprising Keiko still more, her father shook Marcus' hand during their bow, in the American fashion—but in no way disrespectfully, as he had when he'd first arrived.

"For a round-eye, your husband is not so bad," he directed to Keiko.

Marcus said one more traditional farewell, but her father insisted that he be called "Kanaye-*san*" instead of the highly honorific and formal "Oichi-*sama*."

With that, he departed, and Keiko could only stare after him, unsure of what had happened and what it all meant. Her father hadn't forced her to accompany him home or annul her marriage to Marcus. He also hadn't implied she'd been disowned by her family. So what did any of it mean? Was her father ready to accept Christ? Marcus had asked him last night before they went to bed whether he wanted to make that commitment, and her father hadn't quite understood and had refused—but with gentleness that spoke to the fact that he wasn't hardened against the idea in the future. He simply hadn't been ready for such a foreign act and obviously hadn't felt ready even this morning, after his vision and certainty that he'd had a meeting with the one true God.

"I couldn't have predicted this," Keiko murmured in the car. "I thought I knew how my father would react to this whole situation. But he didn't. And now I don't have a clue what happened or what's *going* to happen."

Marcus put a hand on her thigh. "Whatever it is, honey, I no longer think what's going to happen will be bad. Do you?"

"No. No, I don't believe anymore that what happens from this point on will be bad." Hope had sparked, but she wasn't quite ready to trust it yet.

A few weeks later, Marc and Keiko had just gotten back from their trip to Chicago and were preparing to attend the Bible study all his siblings and his father gathered for each Friday evening at the parish. While in The Windy City, they'd cleared out her apartment so someone else could rent it and they'd attended a farewell party thrown by WMMO at their headquarters in Chicago. Though Dan had made a last bid for them both to return to the medical mission field, any location available, his efforts had been half-hearted and more than a little teasing. "You understand that I have to try, don't you? Losing two of our best doctors isn't an easy thing to accept. And if you ever change your minds—"

"Enough said," Marc had interrupted, and all three of them had laughed together heartily.

That trip had been cleansing for Marc, despite the albeit mild panic attack that had hit him within minutes of entering the city. Recalling his mother's dying wish for him, he'd realized that he had no choice but to force himself not to become locked into his homebody instincts while accepting that he wasn't eager to do a lot of traveling anytime in the future. He'd gotten the closure and healing his mother had seemed to realize even before he did that he needed in this area.

Keiko hadn't gotten her closure as yet. Haruki had been calling them often but only to report that their family had said nothing to him...about his father's return, Keiko's broken betrothal and subsequent marriage to an American, and Kanaye Oichi's experience with the Christian God.

"Are we going to tell your family tonight?" Keiko asked him as they took the sidewalk to the parish next door.

"Doctors advise waiting three months before making a public pregnancy announcement."

"Well, we have two doctors here who simply can't wait...even if I am only all of a minute pregnant." She laughed, then hugged him from the side, pouting adorably. "Do we really have to wait three months, Dr. Samuels?"

"There's no way I could, Mrs. Dr. Samuels."

They laughed together and kissed.

Following the Bible study, both of them were stunned when Jay and Ashley announced she was in her second trimester. After her miscarriage around Christmas last year, a short time after they'd married, they'd wanted to wait to say anything about her new pregnancy—at least until they were sure all was going well.

Marc looked at Keiko and knew she was thinking the same thing he was. They would wait to make their own announcement. Unfortunately, they were outed by his sister Samantha, who asked Keiko how her own doctor's appointment yesterday had gone. Keiko had gone to lunch with the women, as usual, and had had to leave earlier than usual. Sam must have talked to Jordan, who'd known Keiko was going to a doctor's appointment. Somehow, two and two had been put together and pregnancy was assumed from there.

"Yes, okay," Marc said, looking at his beaming bride, who gave him a silent go-ahead. "We planned to wait so we wouldn't steal your thunder, but yes, Keiko and I are pregnant, too."

"Only a week pregnant. I knew the first day something was different."

Once more, the hugs and kisses started up and went around the room. "Your mother would be the happiest woman in the world," Marc's father said, embracing him.

The ache that had been covered slightly with all the joy going on in his life flared for a brief moment, but Marc could only believe that his mother *was* happy. She was in heaven with her Lord. If she looked down now, all that she'd imagined for her family would be what she would see.

Marc and Keiko walked home under the moon, holding on to each other. She smiled up at him. "I'm so happy, Marcus."

"So am I."

Her cell phone rang just as they got into the house. "It's Haruki," she announced. She took the call, telling her brother she had him on speakerphone. "What's going on, *nii-chan*?"

"Actually, there's been a development, and I'm not sure what to think about some of it."

"What do you mean?" she demanded.

"First, Yumako just called me. She's marrying Ryu and she couldn't be more thrilled."

"What?" Marc asked in shock.

"She said she wanted that," Keiko said sadly, swallowing in obvious, misplaced guilt. "She's not concerned about her happiness. She only wants to be rich and pampered, to live in luxury."

"I get the feeling our father *gave* her to Ryu," Haruki said, "without telling him that she isn't *you*, Keiko."

"He couldn't."

"He could and I'm sure he did. But Ryu is dying. He's terminally ill, in the final stages of his disease. Who Yumako really is doesn't matter and won't once he dies. She'll be left with a fortune and her obligation to her husband and her family will be finished."

"What if he infects her?" Marc asked.

"I don't think they'll be having...relations. His condition is too deteriorated. When Father approached him about the marriage, Ryu insisted that he didn't want to obligate Keiko to their prior arrangement, knowing he's terminally ill, and so hasn't contacted Grandmother to arrange the marriage ceremony. But Father wouldn't hear of it. Ryu consented so as not to dishonor you and your family, Keiko. The ceremony will be just that—a show to fulfill his duties to our family."

While, at the very least, Marc was glad that their sister wouldn't be relegated to the same disease and a loveless union, it wasn't a situation that inspired gratitude. How could Keiko's father do something like that to his youngest daughter? Could he also be motivated by the money?

"There's one other thing, Keiko," Haruki continued before they'd fully digested everything he'd revealed to this point. "Mother's been asking me since our father returned to Japan what you did to him. I didn't know what she meant until Yumako mentioned that Father has added Christian 'tributes' to our family shrine."

"Tributes? You mean..."

"He's offering tribute to the Christian God *and* to his Shinto deities. It seems Father has incorporated Christianity into all our other religions, and he's asked the rest of the family to join him in worshipping Christ. Of course they agreed. Mother will be calling you soon, Keiko. She wants to discuss meeting Marc-*san*'s family soon. She wants our whole family to go to America and meet Marc's family."

Keiko looked uncertain at the news—Marcus suspected, of her father's idea that he could commit to Christ and other gods, as well as of her family coming here for another visit so soon after the last one.

"She does? Mother wants that?"

"She said after Yumako visited us at the missionary hospital, she suspected you were falling in love with 'the American doctor' and that things would turn out this way, though she told no one. The only thing that truly upset her was finding out that your mother had died recently, Marc-*san*."

"Why would that upset her?" Marc asked softly,

surprised.

"Because she knew Keiko would need a mother and she wanted her to have one in that country."

Keiko's expression turned soft and nostalgic at these words. Marc squeezed her hand, seeing tears glisten in her eyes. She would never have to doubt her mother's feelings for her again.

"You know, Haruki," Marc started, seeing how emotional she was, "I've felt since that second night your father stayed with us that God had His hand on him, maybe on your whole family. If that's true, the Lord will make sure your father banishes the other 'gods'...and your whole family could come to know Christ through this experience."

"Dr. Pollyanna," Haruki teased. "You've never been optimistic before, Marc-*san*. Has my sister had that big of an influence on you?"

"She has, but I'm being serious."

"I believe you're right. This is probably a good time to tell you that Gin has contacted me and wants to talk more about our marriage. She's coming here with the children this weekend."

Haruki signed off with their congratulations and well-wishing, and Keiko murmured, "My father *was* impressed with you, Marcus. I'm convinced that, if not for you, he would have hauled me back to Japan—in his suitcase if he had to, regardless of my wishes."

He shook his head, easing her toward him on the kitchen table bench. "I don't think it had anything to do with me. I think it was you, teddy bear caterpillar turned Tiger moth. You showed your father your true colors, our two worlds collided for him as well, and he backed off because he experienced the truth in a way he couldn't deny. You made an impression on him with your own faith and determination to stand up for what you believe and for us, for our marriage." He enclosed her hands between his and kissed her fingertips. "Every time I think I can't love you more, honey, I find that I can and I do. Our perfect love just keeps happening to me over and over and surprising me more and more."

She hugged him. "All I've ever truly wanted, even before I knew it myself, was to have a life that I can live to the fullest, a life that has purpose. Even if we only had a short time together, I wanted it to mean something. To be worthwhile. And it is. I've found heaven with you, my love. With you, I've found everything I could ever ask for."

*Worlds Collide by Karen Wiesner*

**Also available in the Family Heirlooms Series:**
*Baby, Baby*, Book 1
*Shadow Boxing*, Book 2
*Foolish Games*, Book 3
*Glass Angels*, Book 4
*Shards of Ashley*, Book 5
***Find out more here:***
www.angelfire.com/stars4/kswiesner/fiction9.html

*Return to the quaint little town of Peaceful, Wisconsin,*
*from Karen Wiesner's award-winning Family Heirlooms*
*Series, where you first met and fell in love with these*
*colorful, lovable friends. Now you can read the stories of*
*those secondary characters in an all-new spin-off series.*
*Nuggets of faith can be passed down as heirlooms from*
*friend to friend, heart to heart, soul-mate to soul-mate.*

**Available and coming soon in the Friendship**
**Heirlooms Series:**
*Clumsy Girl's Guide to Falling in Love*, Book 1
*Michael's Angel*, Book 2
*Forever and All That Jazz,* Book 3
*First Comes Love*, Book 4
*Perfect Reflection*, Book 5
*Clumsy Girl's Guide to Having a Baby*, Book 6
*All Good Things*, Book 7
*Clumsy Girl's Guide to Having It All*, Book 8
***Find out more here:***
www.angelfire.com/stars4/kswiesner/fiction9a.html

## About the Author

**Creating realistic, unforgettable characters one story at a time...**

Karen Wiesner is an accomplished author with 106 books published in the past 16 years, which have been nominated for and/or won 126 awards, and has 40 more titles under contract. Karen's books cover such genres as women's fiction, romance, mystery/police procedural/cozy, suspense, paranormal, futuristic, gothic, inspirational, thriller, horror, chick-lit, and action/adventure. She also writes children's books, poetry, and writing reference titles such as her bestseller, *First Draft in 30 Days* and *From First Draft to Finished Novel {A Writer's Guide to Cohesive Story Building}* (now out of print; reissue coming soon in paperback and electronic formats under the title *Cohesive Story Building*). Her third offering from Writer's Digest Books is *Writing the Fiction Series: The Complete Guide for Novels and Novellas,* available now. Her previous writing reference titles focused on non-subsidy, royalty-paying electronic publishing, author promotion, and setting up a promotional group like her own, the award-winning Jewels of the Quill, which she founded in 2003. For more information about Karen's fiction and series, consult her official companion guide *The World of Author Karen Wiesner: A Compendium of Fiction.* Visit her website at http://www.karenwiesner.com. If you would like to receive Karen's free e-mail newsletter, *Karen's Quill,* and become eligible to win her monthly book giveaways, send a blank e-mail to KarensQuill-subscribe@yahoogroups.com.

Made in the USA
Middletown, DE
08 August 2017